Triggadale 2

Lock Down Publications and
Ca$h Presents

Triggadale 2

A Novel by Elijah R. Freeman

Lock Down Publications
P.O. Box 870494
Mesquite, Tx 75187

Visit our website
www.lockdownpublications.com

First Edition August 2019
Printed in the United States of America

Lock Down Publications
Like our page on Facebook: Lock Down Publications @
www.facebook.com/lockdownpublications.ldp
Cover design and layout by: **Dynasty Cover Me**
Book interior design by: **Shawn Walker**
Edited by: **Lauren Burton**

Stay Connected with Us!

Text **LOCKDOWN** to 22828 to stay up-to-date with new releases, sneak peaks, contests and more…

Thank you.

Submission Guideline.

Submit the first three chapters of your completed manuscript to ldpsubmissions@gmail.com, subject line: Your book's title. The manuscript must be in a .doc file and sent as an attachment. The document should be in Times New Roman, double-spaced and in size 12 font. Also, provide your synopsis and full contact information. If sending multiple submissions, they must each be in a separate email.

Have a story but no way to send it electronically? You can still submit to LDP/Ca$h Presents. Send in the first three chapters, written or typed, of your completed manuscript to:

LDP: Submissions Dept
Po Box 870494
Mesquite, Tx 75187

DO NOT send original manuscript. Must be a duplicate.

Provide your synopsis and a cover letter containing your full contact information.

Thanks for considering LDP and Ca$h Presents.

Dedication:

In Loving Memory of La'Treka Lee Green & Willie "AJ" Mosley.

I miss yall already. We all do

Acknowledgements:

First and foremost, I give thanks to Allah, whom without, none of this would even be possible. For he is the Creator of ALL things, and by his will alone, have I been granted this opportunity.
Alhamdullilah!

I thank him for my fiance, Monesa, who has been Hos GREATEST blessing thus far. And baby, thank you for your Love, Loyalty and unfaltering devotion. They say the quickest way to kill a big dream is to tell a small minded individual. When I told you I wanted to write, you became my first fan. I love you for all that you are, and everything you will someday be. My better half for life and death.
I'm forever wit'cha!

Apple Juice, Weezy, Bop, Jaybo...I did it again. Papa Doc! You taught me to be a man, and instilled in my mental that I could do ANYTHING I put my mind to. I been at it since 2014, and been stressin' the fact I told the world I was #TheFutureOfUrbanFiction.
#NowTheyBelieveMe.

To ALL my campaign supporters: Knotlife Marshall (@kls_knotlifeshit), Yung Stuna (@stayup_yungstuna) of Stay Up Or Starve, to the #1 promoter in Clay Co. and the Metro Atlanta area- Khadija (@theoriginalratchet), The T-shirt King (@the_shirtking) out there on the west coast, April Freeman, Uno, Kimberly Flounory, my favorite cuzzo's Dana and T'quan, RMP Graphixx, Moe (stampd_monefa), my boi Troy (@aveboy_t) from uptop, my Real-Right cousin Trese.

My faithful cousin 6, my Trinity Park gwallas (Kel Ru•Sebastian•Lil D), the RCK Don himself Juju (voice_the_truth), 220 Jackboi (@ygsicario), 6kingsclothing in Columbus Ohio. To the new "Face of Riverdale" Drewski Gottem (@drupac_220), my "Day-One" right-hand-man with this publishing vision Chris Exom (@_nojewelry), and I can't forget about the trenches and everybody #BehindTheWall - I sincerely appreciate your efforts, both major and minor. I don't care if it was something as minimal as a Like, a post in your story, or simply you taking your time out to brainstorm marketing ideas with me. I don't take it for granted. No actin is too small. They all add up over time. Thank you.

I want to give a special shout-out to Gucci & Georgia Hudson, and Keyera Stewart. Action express priority, and y'all go out y'all way to support me, always the first to pop up with copies of my work. That's love.

And yea...I see you Sham (Thomas Habersham- author of "Circle of Death"). Thanks for the oppotunity that got me here. Ca$H...Salute! LDP on top, and shall never fall.

Free my brother, Takeoff Montana!!!

"No man is whole of himself. His friends are the other half..."

-Unknown

PROLOGUE

Huncho sat behind the defendant bench, awaiting the jurors' return, in a black Giorgio Armani suit. He was back up the road on appeal and had been in and out of the courtroom fighting for his life for the last three months. Today would end it all. By nightfall, he'd be a free man or appealing the Superior Court's decision to a higher power. Needless to say, he was nervous and it showed.

To his right, in a black Hugo Boss suit, was his attorney, Kendall Leonard. He leaned in to whisper, "Relax, man, we got this."

"How you figure that?" Huncho said. "You see the way this old racist-ass white man keeps lookin' at me?"

"Who?"

"The judge."

Mr. Leonard chuckled, adjusting his glasses. "That's the least of your concerns. Look how long they're taking. It's when they come right back that you have something to be worried about. Take my word."

And he would.

Mr. Leonard was the best of the best, Clayton County's finest. He was so good that Huncho's mother made it her business to see to it that he represented her baby. The fact that he was black made her all the more determined. At the time, he was riding a winning streak of fifty-six.

That's where it ended.

Despite his expertise, Huncho was convicted, proof that Clayton County had a personal vendetta against him. Mr. Leonard was so upset that he was doing his appeal for free, and he had gone more than out of his way to prove that all evidence against his client was circumstantial, creating reasonable doubt.

Behind them, spectators were scarce, scattered here and there throughout the rows of benches. Camry and his mother would've shown their support, but he was keeping his court dates low-key. Outside his mother, no one knew his appeal had been granted. Asked about being back up the road, he told people he was back fighting miscellaneous charges he'd caught while on the run. Knowing his stilo, they went for it without question.

A hush fell over the courtroom as the jury returned. Huncho's heart was beating fast as he watched the foreman prepare to announce the jury's decision.

The judge cleared his throat. "Has the jury reached a verdict?"

The foreman stood. "Um, yes, Your Honor. We, the jury, find the defendant not guilty of all charges."

Huncho and Mr. Leonard looked at each other in excitement. Both were truly elated. What Huncho didn't know was that Mr. Leonard knew all along what the outcome would be. The judge and prosecutor had been paid off. That was one of the reasons his retainer fee was so high. And as quiet as it was kept, that was how the game was being played.

After shaking hands, the bailiff escorted him back to the holding cell, where he stayed, bucking on going back to the dorm to await his release. The last thing he needed was his freedom announced. He could see the uproar now. Before being released, he dressed out in a grey, white, and black Coogi 'fit, some black and grey Jordan 4's, and a black hoody.

Outside, the courthouse the sky was a cloudy grey. People were in and out as he scanned the scene for Mr. Leonard. Apparently there were some papers he had yet to sign. He stood at the top of the steps, overlooking the crowded parking lot, until he spotted his attorney mid-way through the lot, leaned up against an all-white Audi. He made his way down the stairs, taking in the modest traffic on Tara Boulevard as he descended.

"So what's the first thing you're gonna do now that you're free?"

"Ain't no tellin'." Huncho signed the last document. "Matta fact, mind if I use yo' phone?"

"No problem." Mr. Leonard pulled a Blackberry from his pocket and handed it over.

Huncho dialed a number and waited. They answered on the third ring.

"Yo."

"Purp?"

"Yeah, who is?" There was shuffling and moving around. "Hello? What's up, who this?"

"Huncho."

"What the fuck! Hold up, where you at?"

"Right outside the courthouse, my nigga."

"Ain't no way!" Purp yelled in excitement. "You done pulled it off."

"Damn right. I gotta holla at you 'bout that suit and tie, though." That was their lingo for "talk business".

"Okay, cool, just get at me when you get settled. Same place. I'm still here."

"Say no mo'."

"A'ight, one."

"One."

Huncho hung up, handing Mr. Leonard his phone back.

"Hitting the ground running, are we?"

Huncho eyed him suspiciously. "What you mean?"

"I know everyone there is to know who dibbles and dabbles in illegalities in Clayton County, Mr. Blanding. Tell Purp

I said hey." Mr. Leonard reached for the driver's side door then and stopped. He pulled his business card out of his pocket and he handed it over. "Take this. You're gonna need it if you plan on getting your hands dirty. You can't outrun the law forever. A word of advice. Get in, stack your bread, and then get out. That's what I did." Mr. Leonard hopped in his Audi and rode off.

Huncho pulled his hoody over his head and stuffed his hands in its pockets. After taking a deep breath, he started off up the block toward the C-Tran bus stop. As he walked, he thought about what Mr. Leonard had said, but quickly dismissed it. He was dead-ass right. Huncho couldn't take that from him. But this go 'round, he was living by his own creed.

Get rich or die talking.

CHAPTER 1

Huncho got off at the light on Highway 85 and began his trek down Lake Ridge Parkway. Throughout his bid, dreams of this day had been frequent. In them he would come home, surprising Camry, who, elated to see him, would cry tears of joy. His baby girl, Zakayla, would scream, "Daddy" and run and jump in his arms. He'd swing her around, stopping only to shower her angelic face with kisses. She was the spitting image of her mother, with his eyes and attitude.

As he walked, he prepared himself for memory lane, a road that often proved bumpy with potholes the size of houses. Garden Lake Apartments. He stopped at the mouth of the entrance. As he stared at the sign, he thought of Katrina. Last he heard, she got out of prison and moved up top somewhere. No one had seen or heard from her since.

Southside Queens was no more. Missy was the last official Queen, and she stopped putting in work a long time ago. He bumped into someone down the road that said she relocated to Douglasville, and had two kids. He wasn't sure how true it was, but he couldn't imagine Missy as a mother. She was too tom-boyish.

He pushed on, meditating on life's randomness. You never knew where you would find yourself five years from now, or hell, five years from then. Life was just crazy like that sometimes…or so he guessed.

The traffic on Lake Ridge Parkway was lite, with cars passing by every now and then. Up ahead, a white Malibu headed his way. As it approached, he got a better look at its interior, making his heart race. It was full of clique poppas and had a lime green bandanna tied to its rearview mirror.

The driver, he recognized.

Marko.

Remembering that the Mafia and Squad beef was no more, he exhaled. Nard was a rat. Having been apprehended with a hot strap, he had cut a deal with Ellis. He hadn't wanted to believe it, but when Jayvo showed him his discovery packet, he could deny it no longer. It was in black and white.

Since the war popped the night he was jumped, many Mafiosos didn't feel right warring in the name of a snitch. A Squad affiliate was taking off on the rap tip, and Hit Squad wasn't feeling the beef, either. They made an executive decision to settle their differences. They were even doing songs together. The scene was changing. Everything was about money now.

Before long he came to a vast lake that served as a centerpiece for the neighborhood. He stepped closer until he was standing atop a hill, on a black cement trail that circled the lake. He took a deep breath through his nose, exhaling heavily out his mouth. The breeze was strong and refreshing. He ran his hand over his even chop, still unaccustomed to his dread-free scalp.

Huncho stared out across the lake, wishing Flame was there to share in his victory against the system. It was supposed to have been theirs. Every day he missed his nigga, and sometimes, he still couldn't believe he was gone. Spitting in the grass, he noticed grey letters spray painted on the trail beneath him. He stepped back.

2-DUB

Huncho continued on to Briar Crest, the housing subdivision off Lake Ridge where Camry resided. She and Zakayla had been staying there almost a year now. He followed the numbers on the mailboxes until he came to a white house. He walked up the driveway, bypassing a burgundy Toyota Corolla.

Once at the door, he knocked. No answer. Knocking once more, only to be ignored, he tried the knob and to his surprise, it turned. He pushed the door open and what he saw blew the fuck out of him.

The entire house was cluttered. As he walked through, he saw dirty clothes in the laundry room that had yet to be washed. Unwashed dishes filled the kitchen sink. The living room floor could use a vacuum. On one of the end tables was a framed family picture he, Zakayla, and Camry took at visitation during his bid. He reached for it, but something else caught his eye.

A stack of mail.

All through the stack was one overdue bill after another. Credit cards. Cable. Utilities. You name it. With each bill, he grew hotter and hotter. It was bigger than debt. Camry had been lying to him, claiming everything was under control. His baby girl had probably been labeled a peon, and forced to go without all because of her mother's pride. He had no idea she was in a bind of this magnitude, but seeing the reality of the situation left him unnerved.

Camry walked into the living room, guiding Zakayla by the hand, coaching and encouraging her. After realizing she wasn't alone, she started to scream until she locked eyes with Huncho, truly shocked.

"But…how?" Zakayla stared at Huncho, confused.

She looked up at Camry. "Daddy?"

A smile started at the corners of her mouth, but stopped when Huncho held up the stack of envelopes.

"When were you going to tell me the truth?"

"I-I-umm." Lost for words, she knelt, scooping up Zakayla.

"You what!" He threw the stack of envelopes at her. "You've been lying to me!"

Zakayla cried.

"Daldrick, stop, you're scaring her." Camry began bouncing Zakayla to sooth her.

"How much debt you in?"

"Daldrick, I can handle it," Camry's eyes welled with tears. "Shit is just hard right now. I'ma catch up." She wiped at her tears, bouncing Zakayla to avoid the question. Knowing another lie would only make matters worse, she confessed. "A few thousand." Camry broke down. "I'm about to lose my car and I'm short on this month's rent."

Huncho's heart ached as he watched the tears flow from her eyes. Gently, he took Zakayla from her arms and guided her to the sofa, where they sat down and discussed the situation. After the bills were added up, the total debt was thirteen thousand and some change. Camry hadn't realized she was in that much debt and staring at the figures on the paper brought a new set of tears.

Huncho sat in deep thought. He was so bemused that he didn't even notice Camry grab Zakayla and leave the room. He ran his hand down his face. Something had to be done. He couldn't believe his luck. Not even a full twenty-four hours in the free world and he was already under pressure. Even if he had intended to do the right thing, this would've offset that decision, he was sure. He got up, grabbed Camry's keys off the kitchen counter, and headed out the front door. Camry returned to the living room to no Huncho. Rushing to the window, she was just in time to see Huncho pulling away in her car.

Club 5-4-3 was one of Atlanta's premiere strip clubs. It boasted some of the baddest chicks in the city, and a VIP list on which were some of the biggest names in the entertainment industry. On any given night you could spot a Royce on the scene. It wasn't nothing to see a Phantom curbside out front. Benz's. Bentley's. Lambo's. All sitting high end in the valet parking. Not to mention the long line of "super having its" outside.

Purp, the club's owner, was a Benji Family Capo. Hood millionaire. For years, the Feds chased him, but could never establish enough probable cause to get an indictment. His money was covered by a multimillion-dollar lawsuit he received after suing the DeKalb County Sheriff's Department for police brutality. The Feds weren't fooled, though. They knew he was still connected to the streets.

In his office he entertained two brothers, Ricardo and Carlos Espinoza. They were in town from the west coast for the BET Awards and were feeling like royalty amid the plushness of his realm.

The all-white carpet. The room Jacuzzi. The two sharks swimming around the six-hundred-gallon wall aquarium. The wet bar. The strippers. The *Scarface*-like security monitors, showing different parts of the club, inside and outside.

The room was full of blueberry kush smoke. The three sexy Asian dancers kept their cups full at all times. Purp sat behind his desk while Ricardo and Carlos lounged on the leather sectional with their own personal bikini-and-stiletto-wearing waitress. Ricardo was a stout Hispanic with long, wavy, jet-black hair. Carlos was of the same ethnicity, only mid-height and skinny, sporting a crewcut.

These were no ordinary migos, though. They were the plug. The way. Weed. Coke. Pills. Whatever! They were connected. He'd known them even before the settlement. The only thing that had changed was the quantity he purchased each trip.

"So Purp, when you coming out west to open a spot?" Ricardo took a sip of his Remy VSOP. "We need something like this in Cali."

Carlos rubbed his face against the soft flesh of the dancer sitting on his lap.

"Yo, I love Cali but y'all be havin' them earthquakes and shit. I can't get used to no shit like that. Now, what y'all can do is send some of them exotic bitches to work for me so when y'all be in town y'all can still feel like y'all at home."

"Bullshit! I feel at home now with these Georgia Peaches!" Carlos turned his drink up. "Ahhh! It don't get no better than this, ain't that right, mami?"

The petite, honey-dipped dancer snuggled next to him, all smiles. "You ain't seen nothing yet, baby. You know what they say about us down south girls!"

Everyone laughed.

Purp's office phone rang aloud, interrupting the kick-it. Frowning, he glanced its way. He had made it very clear he was not to be disturbed, and was now clearly frustrated. Ricardo and Carlos carried on, whispering to the dancers. Purp shooed the dancers sitting on his desk towards the other females, then answered.

"This better be important."

"A guy I've never seen before insists on speaking to you. Claims you'd let him back if you knew he was out here." Clyde peeked at Huncho through the Vatican-style water fountain. "I told him you weren't here, but he still ain't left."

"Think he's a Fed?"

"Naw, brah, this a street nigga all day." He watched Huncho move casually toward the bar. "Says his name's Huncho."

Purp spun, facing the monitors behind him. "Tall, slim cat, with long dreads?"

"Tall and slim, but his hair's cut low. He's sitting at bar number two ordering two blue mu'fuckas. What's up, sic the wolves on him?"

Purp found Huncho on the monitors. "Naw, bring him back." He hung up the phone, dismissed the three dancers, then turned to Ricardo and Carlos. "I got somebody for y'all to meet. Straight goon!"

Huncho was led back to Purp's office, sandwiched between Clyde and Tank, two big, black, mountainous men dressed in black cargo pants and black shirts with "security" and "5-4-3" on the front and back in white letters and all-black One's on their feet. Tank had cornrolls while Clyde rocked a bald head. Huncho mugged him, and it didn't go unnoticed by anyone in the room.

"What's up, my nigga, what the fuck?" Purp stepped from behind his desk, embracing Huncho. "Uh huh, they done fucked up now!" Purp stepped back and threw his guard up. "What's up? Get right, li'l nigga."

Huncho squared up. "Run up, then, nigga. What's up!"

They shadow boxed a little, then hit each other with the pound.

"So how'd you do it?"

"Simple." Huncho shrugged. "I beat it on appeal."

"Yeah, my nigga. I can dig it. But let me introduce you to some friends of mine, while I fix you a drink."

Introductions were made, impressions were given, and conversations were held as blunts circulated. Purp could sense something was weighing on Huncho's mind. So after Ricardo and Carlos left, he decided to see what it was. There was a reason for him popping up out of the blue, demanding to see him during day shift at his club.

"So what brought you out the woods to holla at ya boy?" Purp lit a Newport. "Everything a'ight with ya, ain't it?"

"Hell naw, shit ugly den a mu'fucka. I ain't eatin', my nigga. I'm tryna eat." Huncho spread his arms out. "I ain't got shit! Nothin'. I ain't got shit, but I know I can grind."

"What you need?" Purp popped some gum in his mouth, and began chewing. "You name it. A job. Some work. Pills. Money. Anything you want, I'll make it happen."

Two days later, Huncho had Camry drive him to a house in Stone Mountain and drop him off. Less than ten minutes later, he reemerged from the garage, backing out in a black Yukon, in the back of which was fifty pounds of popcorn bud. At five hundred a pop, the ticket was twenty-five thousand dollars. That meant if he sold all twenty-five for a stack, fifty thousand would be his to pocket. He couldn't lose.

He pulled into the driveway and saw Camry sitting out front talking to their neighbor. He unloaded the two big wheel boxes and took them into the house. Inside was thick, plastic-wrapped weed with extra layers of Saran around it. The thick plastic was the packaging of an outdoor tent and had been vacuum sealed to compress the bails. Styrofoam chips were inside to keep them from moving along with Bounty dryer sheets to keep the dogs from hitting. The last layer of Saran before getting to the plastic was filled with coffee grains. They spilled from the wrap.

After busting down both bails, he was setting fistfuls on the kitchen counter as Camry walked in. Upon seeing all the weed, she stomped out toward their bedroom. Huncho waved her off, dismissing her reaction. There was money to be made. He broke bails into pounds, flipping numbers around in his head.

"If a nigga wants more than one, he can get 'em for eight-hundred. Five or better, six-fifty," he reasoned. "And nothing less than a QP. I gotta get me a tool ASAP too!"

***

"Damn, shawdy, this shit smokin'. Where you get it from?" Thugga released a tirade of coughs, exhaling the potent smoke. "This that gangsta!"

Eyes bloodshot red, Rock smiled as he played XBOX.

Rock and Thugga were Flame's younger cousins who stayed off Scott Road. Neither had been in the streets when Huncho and Flame were going hard. They were students at Riverdale High School until Rock was kicked out, having been caught red-handed with a strap and some weed in his locker. Thugga followed not long after for participation in gang activity.

They were both young. They were both 2-DUB. They were both troublesome.

"Shoota fucked with me," Rock said.

"Mafia, Shoota?"

"Hell yeah. He say Huncho back on the move." Rock paused the game, reaching for the blunt. "I ain't e'en know he got out, but Shoota said he touched down and he 'bout to crank the Mafia back up."

Thugga rubbed his hands together. "What's up, they fuckin' with us?"

He had always looked up to Huncho from the stories and rumors he heard around the way. He was officially idolized the day he made the news while on the run for murder. Thugga began claiming the Mafia, making it his business to make it known that Flame was his cousin.

Rock dabbed the blunt out in the ash tray, blowing smoke out his nose. "I think so. Shoota ain't say too much, but that's the impression I get."

"Shiiid, it's on then!" Thugga leaped off the couch. "Where he stayin', back at The Spot?"

"I don't know. I told Shoota to holla at him for me." Rock passed the blunt.

Later that day, Thugga and Rock met up with Shoota to cop some more weed, and, to their surprise, Huncho's number.

Back at home, Rock called the number they were given. Huncho answered on the third ring, giving them directions to where he was. Forty minutes later, they were pulling up behind the Yukon.

Huncho gave each of them a pound of weed, making it clear he needed his money within a week. What made them leave with a smile was Huncho stamping them as Southside Mafia. They would be his lieutenants. Shoota. Rock. Thugga. And Woadie, the prince of the DUB. All they had to do was stay loyal.

It was official.

2-DUB Mafia.

They were official.

CHAPTER 2

Two and a half weeks had passed since Purp blessed Huncho with the weed. Twenty-five stacks. Paid in full. He grinded day and night, sweating hard, and was down to the six pounds he'd copped for himself and the sixteen thousand for his re-up. He paid off some of Camry's bills and she eased up on him about being back in the game. Now she was looking to start school at Emory University. He was still far from where he wanted to be, but first and foremost, he had to get his money right. Money brought you power, and respect was just something that came with the package.

Thugga, Shoota, and Rock turned out to be major assets to his plan.

With his face back on the scene, rumors of him being free were no longer rumors. The streets were talking. Some out of admiration. Some out of respect. Some out of fear.

He wouldn't use fear to overcome his enemies, though. No, he would use his team instead. Never again would he be the face on the front line. He had put in his work, paid his dues and then some. It was time for his soldiers to step to the plate.

He finished rubber-banding twenty grand on the living room sofa and called Purp. Camry walked in. Upon seeing all the folded knots on the table, she hugged him from behind and planted a kiss on his cheek. She knew he was getting money, but damn. She ain't know it was like that. He shook her off and relit the blunt, resting it in the ashtray.

"Wuddup, yo." Purp answered.

Camry mushed him playfully and walked out.

Huncho tried to grab that ass, but missed. He smiled. "Coolin', my nigga. What's good with you, brah?"

"Shit, out here in Cali fuckin' 'round at the studio with one of my artists. Tryna get 'em signed. What the business is, though? Tell me somethin' good."

At the mention of Cali, Huncho felt a wave of disappointment. He had six pounds left to his name, and four of them were just waiting to get dropped off. The thought of being dry had him kicking himself for not following his instincts. He could've re-upped earlier in the week but didn't, wanting to have enough to pay Purp off and skin down for his own pack this go 'round. Had he foreseen this circumstance, he would've stuck to the script and caught Purp on the back end. Being without product was bad business. Weed clientele had a tendency to switch plugs when they felt their source was unreliable.

Huncho chose his words carefully due to the phone. "Shiiid, I needed to see ya!"

"Oh, you through with that track already?" Purp replied, reading him loud and clear.

"Yeah, it's a wrap. When you gon' be back in town? I'm tryna lay another one ASAP."

"Can I hit you back at this number?"

"Sho'nuff."

"A'ight, keep ya line clear."

Huncho placed twenty-five stacks in a bag and ten of his sixteen in a separate one. He would cop his own work with ten and put six up.

Camry returned with a bag of popcorn and a tall glass of Sprite.

He handed her six thousand. "Put that up. Don't touch it 'less I tell you to."

"Yes suh, Massa," she replied, imitating a slave. "Anything else ya need, Massa, just let me know and I's a come runnin'."

He laughed. "Girl, go 'head on with that shit!"

He received the call back from Purp and headed to the location he'd been given, a residence in Fayetteville. He pulled into the driveway of a granite house and the garage door rose, revealing a sexy Latina holding a cocaine-white, red nose pit on a leash. She was light-skinned and short. The shirt she rocked left her flat stomach exposed, diamond navel ring on fleek, as she waved him into the garage. She slid it shut behind him and approached the truck, her curve-hugging shorts gripping her pussy lips.

Now that she was closer, he realized she was even more beautiful than he originally perceived. Cherub cheeks. Creamy soft skin. A pretty smile accentuated with deep dimples. She reminded him of Cuban Lust, a model he'd seen in several *Black Men* magazines during his bid. In fact, the two of them could be easily mistaken for sisters.

He stepped out of the truck, eyeing the dog, who stood at attention, watching him. She tugged at the chain and ordered the dog to sit.

"She won't bother you." Her Spanish accent was heavy. "C'mon in, follow me. And my name is Yara."

He followed the 5'4" beauty into the house, taking in the way her ass bounced with each step. He could tell she was putting an added sway to her hips. She unleashed the pit in a room at the end of the hall, then continued on to the kitchen, where two big wheel boxes, much like the ones he picked up in Stone Mountain, awaited him in the middle of the floor.

"They just got here today. You're more than welcome to check them before you leave if you like. But first, do you have something for me?"

Huncho dumped twenty-five stacks in the middle of the table. Yara stepped to the table and picked up a bundle, thumbing through it.

"Twenty-five, right?"

"Yeah, it's all there and then some. I brought an extra ten to cop my own weight."

Yara looked surprised. "Purp spoke nothing of this."

"I didn't want to mention it over the phone. I planned to handle it here, but if you're uncomfortable, maybe you should hit his line and let him know what's up."

She thought for a moment, scrutinizing him as if her eyes held the power to distinguish bullshit from trustworthy. Using her middle finger, she whisked a strand of hair behind her ear.

"One moment, please." She gathered up the twenty-five stacks and left the room, returning a minute later with her phone pressed to her ear.

Huncho listened to the unilateral conversation. It was obvious that Yara was receiving instructions. Three minutes later, she ended the call with a smile.

"Okay! This is what he said!" Clasping her hands, she smacked her lips. "Give me the ten G's you have and only bring back fifteen on this package, and when he returns, the two of you will talk business."

Huncho gave her the money and moments later, he loaded the boxes into the Yukon. Engaging him in conversation, she walked with him, waiting for him to depart. He climbed in the driver seat and reached to close the door, but she stepped between.

She bit her bottom lip seductively. "It'll be a few days before he gets back in town. Why don't you take my number and give me a call when you have some spare time?"

Huncho looked her up and down. "No offense, but it's all business with me." He closed the door and started the engine.

After he backed out of the driveway and pulled off, she let the garage down and went back inside to call Purp. He answered on the second ring.

"Yo?"

"He didn't go for it. Said it's all business with him. I think he can be trusted."

"That's what's up. Get the money out the house and be at the airport at six."

***

Huncho's name was ringing in the streets, despite the fact he was rarely seen. Throwback Mafiosos were wondering why he hadn't hit them up. Some of them had turned state witnesses against their co-defendants on cases they caught while Huncho was fighting his murder charge. Four Frontline Mafiosos had been convicted under the Georgia Gang Act Law and sent to prison. All because of people with loose lips.

Like Nard.

With Huncho, and most of the original Mafia off the street, Nard moved to Lovejoy and took it upon himself to recruit new members, making his own squad, Trigga Mafia Cutthroats - or T.M.C., for short. Claiming 11,000 Block - or 11 Stackz, as they called it - they were thought to be a new chapter under the Mafia banner until the Frontline sent word back to the streets that Trigga Mafia was in no way affiliated with Southside Mafia. Neither was Nard. It was declared.

There was only one Mafia.

Nard had been prosperous in the cocaine business, serving up the south side. He had close to fifty members hoodwinked, believing they were rockin' with a solid nigga, when truth be told, there was nothing solid about him. Sad part about it was there were a lot of real niggas in Trigga Mafia. Nard just had them fooled, a fact that if ever revealed would ruin everything he worked so hard to acquire.

Nard had heard that Huncho was back on the street and felt it could be a threat to his credibility. Loss of street cred meant loss of followers, which ultimately added up to his money coming up short, and he wasn't having that. He had to prevent his face from being tainted at all cost.

He was riding down Flint River Road in his white and grey Range Rover, listening to a recent T.M.C. track called, "Hoez Ain't Shit," when his phone rang. Checking the screen, he saw it was his homeboy Dru.

He turned the music down. "Whaddup, brah?"

"Boy! Guess who I just saw? You ain't gon' believe this shit!"

Nard was unconcerned. "Who?"

"Ya boy, Huncho! Nigga riding a new Yukon on factory rims. He ain't see me, though."

At the mention of Huncho, Nard muted the music. "Oh yeah? Where you seen shawdy at?"

"Leaving that nigga Rock's house, and he had Shoota in the truck wit' em."

"Shoota...Shoota," Nard said to himself, trying to put a face with the name.

"You know. The nigga that claim he Mafia, but don't fuck with us."

"Oh, yeah, that Shoota!" Nard remembered Shoota from the days of the original Southside Mafia. He was one of the few that had stayed loyal, choosing to ride his time in the county, which ended up being eighteen months. "So...them niggas back at it, huh?"

"I guess so, but peep this. Remember Flame?"

"Yeah, what about him."

"How 'bout his cousin's Rock and Thugga screamin' 2-DUB Mafia now."

Nard laughed uneasily. "Naw, them niggas ain't Mafia. We the mu'fuckin' Mafia!" He sounded like Tupac on "Hit 'Em Up." "Next time you hear them niggas screamin' Mafia, mash they shit in!"

"Say no mo'," Dru said. "Aye, they gettin work from the nigga too!"

"Straight up?"

"That's on 11 Stackz, brah. He frontin' them all a few pounds to work."

"Wait, how the hell you know?"

"Deductive reasoning, nigga. They ain't been had no weight. Now all of a sudden he touchdown and they on. I had to have jumped off the porch yesterday!"

"Look, I'ma have to hit ya back. I'm 'bout to run in the barbershop and get a cut." Nard turned into the KFC plaza parking lot. "But find out what you can and we'll chop it up when I'm through. I got something for their ass. We gon' show 'em who the real Mafia is."

As Nard got his hair cut, he thought about Huncho. If he wanted to keep his place in the game, he would have to eliminate him before he began to rise. There was one solution to the problem, and that was it.

He had to stop Huncho before he got started.

***

Thugga was posted in 12 Oaks, where he was trapping out Smoker Pam's apartment. Besides the weed, he sold hard, something he'd done since he was thirteen years old. He was now fifteen with shoulder-length dreads that hung freely in his face. Brown-skinned, he stood 5'6", rocking top and bottom pull-out golds.

Following in his cousin's footsteps, he was quick to bust his guns and 2-DUB Mafia with a passion. He was making it his life's reason for breathing, especially since Huncho had put him down.

He sat on the couch, smoking and bagging up weed as "Block Boi Bounce" played from the stereo. Rock was usually at the apartment with him, but was making a run for Huncho, dropping off a few pounds. He decided to stay in the trap since he just re-upped on his work.

A knock at the door brought Pam from the back, where she had been getting high with another smoker. She answered the door and let in a smoker named Leroy.

"Whaddup, Leroy, how much you got for me?" Thugga was at the dining room table stuffing weed in little baggies.

Leroy pushed his hand down in his pocket. "I got seven dollars and some change, but I'll have a li'l more later on."

"Let me get the seven dollars. Give Pam the change." Thugga stuck his hand out. "Since I'm takin' this change, you is gon' smoke it with her, right?"

"Yeah, yeah, you know I was gon' look out for the house lady," he lied joyfully. "It's two boys out there that want some of that reefer, too."

Thugga served Leroy and went to handle business with his weed customers outside. At the sight of the two figures dressed in all black, he got a bad vibe and eased the Glock from his lower back, flicking the safety off.

"Aye, what's up shawdy? Y'all looking for that thrax?" he asked.

The one on the passenger side spoke. "Yeah, is it smokin'?"

"It's some gangsta-ass popcorn mid." Thugga fingered

the trigger on the Glock. He could feel something was about to jump off, but his gangsta wouldn't let him back down. If it was drama they were bringing, that's what he lived for. "So, what y'all tryna do?"

"We tryna get a zip, if the ticket right," the driver said. "I need a dollar."

"A dollar! Shiiid, I ain't been paying but eighty from my folks."

"My nigga, I ain't ya folks. So what's the business, brah?"

The driver looked over the top of the car at his partna. "Well, shit, bring it on then, shawdy. If it's some of that thrax, we'll fuck with ya."

Thugga went in the house, fixed up an ounce, and came back out. He noticed the one on the passenger side was now sitting on the hood of the car with his arms folded across his chest to conceal the pistol he was holding. The driver opened the door and stood one foot in, one foot out of the car. Thugga kept his eyes on the one on the hood. As he reached the sidewalk, the guy on the hood looked from side to side, then slid off the car with the pistol down at his side. Thugga raised his tool and let loose.

BWA! BWA! BWA!

Two bullets pierced his gut, and a third hit his shoulder as he turned and tried to run. The driver opened fire on Thugga, causing him to back step towards the apartment door.

BWA! BWA! BWA! BWA! BWA!

The Glock .45 kicked in Thugga's hand until the chamber stayed cocked back, signaling an empty clip. The driver used the few seconds to get in the car and reach over to open the door for his partna, who was clutching at his stomach. The passenger fell in across the seat and the driver sped off with the passenger door open, the wounded robber's feet hanging out. Thugga came back out of the apartment with a fresh clip, letting off shots at the car as it fled the scene.

At the sound of the sirens, Thugga ran back inside, gathered his things, and fled the scene on foot. Dipping across Roy Huie, he threw his work in some bushes and called Rock and Shoota. Rock was on his way from Newnan, but Shoota was in the area and came to his rescue. Five minutes later, he pulled up and Thugga hopped in his car, explaining what had happened on the way to Shoota's crib in Roundtree Forest.

"I'm tellin' you, I ain't never seen these niggas before." He pulled on a Newport and blew the smoke out the window. "We'll know who it was soon. I wet one of they ass up."

"Well, shiiid, just lay low at my spot tonight. Twelve gone be hot as a mu'fucka after this shit." They slowed to a stop at the traffic light at the four-way by Riverdale High School. "You think Pam gon' say something?"

"I doubt it. Without me and Rock paying her rent, her ass'll be out on the street."

At Shoota's crib they sat on the porch, smoked a couple blunts, and chilled until later joined by Rock. They told Huncho what happened and wrote it off as a lick gone wrong. What they didn't know was that it was far from a random lick.

The two robbers had been sent by Nard.

CHAPTER 3

"You can get 'em at two hundred fifty apiece if you are buying ten or better. The catch is getting them back to Georgia," Purp said. "I've been fucking with the mail, but that shit risky than a mu'fucka. Niggas been getting knocked left and right lately. The Feds been letting the shit come through and as soon as a nigga sign that paper, they rush his ass. That's trafficking across state lines, the worst case you can have." He passed Huncho the blunt.

It had been two months since Huncho had walked into Club 5-4-3 all those nights ago, and within that time, he had progressed considerably. No longer did he accept fronts from Purp. He was now copping his own. Purp gave him the Cali connect so he could deal with Ricardo and Carlos directly. As they rode through Buckhead in Purp's Bentley GT Coupe, he gave Huncho the game on copping large amounts of weed from across the map.

"So, say I don't wanna fuck with the mail and wanna take my chances on the road? 'Cause that mail shit sound shaky to me."

Purp shrugged, nodding as he contemplated his next words. "The highways are fucked up. You know about 95 being the main pipeline from Miami? Well, Highway 10 is twice as hot. 10 runs through Arizona, New Mexico, Texas, and Louisiana. The checkpoints are unavoidable. You gotta travel 10 to get home. The worst checkpoint is in Texas, just beyond Louisiana. The Mexicans move a lot of coke through there coming from Mexico. Not to mention all the weed coming from Arizona."

He went on to explain how state troopers operated at checkpoints, and Huncho decided to take his chances with the mail. Purp offered to provide a female to sign for his first package if he was willing to pay her out of his own pocket.

At two hundred-fifty a pound, he was copping fifty. There was no looking back once he got them. He figured if he sold each pound for eight hundred dollars a pop, he was looking at a thirty-thousand-dollar profit. Music to his ears.

In return for the weed plug, Huncho agreed to cop his coke from Purp. They were locked in. He had already copped two bricks. Until the time was right, he would sit on them.

They ate at Justin's and headed back to Riverdale. Huncho got in his two-tone Dodge Camaro. The top half was black, the bottom half grey. He had returned the Yukon to Purp weeks ago. On his way back to the crib, he called his boy Shoota to see if he was up to steppin' out that night. He was. Thugga, Rock, and Woadie were as well.

As he drove, he thought about how crazy it was that just last year he was in chain gang serving a life sentence. A lot of young niggas his age got down the road and just gave up.

Not him.

His nigga D-Day, also serving life, was waiting on his appeal to go through. He felt bad that he'd been convicted because it had been for Tevo's murder. Ellis didn't care who went down for what. Southside Mafia was a gang. Everyone was guilty.

Huncho thought about his four homeboys who were all serving time for gang activity: D-Day; Dumbway; Kasaan; Fred. He missed them all. Thinking of them made him pull over at a gas station and get them each a fifty dollar money order.

At home, Camry was cooking and Zakayla was playing on the floor. Huncho scooped her up, went over to Camry, and hugged her from behind, kissing her on the neck. She smiled. Ever since he caught her up on all the bills and straightened her credit so she could begin medical school, she had been a new person. The sex was better, they didn't argue, and she didn't trip when he left the house. She even drove for him on some of his runs when he had big deliveries.

"What's that you cooking?" he asked. "That shit smelling good as hell!"

"Lemon pepper wings. You want some fries with 'em?"

He tossed a giggling Zakayla in the air playfully. "Yeah, that'll be cool."

"D-Day called. I was gon' call you on three way, but his time ran out on the phone."

Huncho paused, getting serious. "He say when he was gon' call back?"

"Tomorrow. Some girl gave him a three-way."

I gotta put some money on the phone, Huncho thought.

"And you got some mail in there by the computer."

He went in the living room, carrying Zakayla. Seeing it was from his homeboy Dumbway, he smiled. Dumbway was a part of the crew that had been sent to prison for the pawn shop heist, the Mafiosos he loved like brothers, the ones who'd put him down in the Mafia. He sat Zakayla on the couch beside him and opened the letter, reading with a smile.

Dumbway talked about coming home and what they would be doing once they all got back together. He asked for pictures. Asked what was going on in the streets. Wanted to know if he'd seen his brother Longway. Then he told Huncho to stay free, ending with a reminder to keep the Mafia alive.

Huncho wrote Dumbway back, ate, then got dressed to go out. He put on a purple Black Label polo shirt and black jeans. He rocked a black fitted over his twist, which he wasn't quite ready to reveal, and on his feet he wore black Polo boots. Once he was ready, he picked Shoota up. Thugga, Rock, and Woadie were in Woadie's red Mazda.

The four of them pulled up to Magic City in two separate cars, searching for a parking space. After finding none, Huncho decided to take them to Club 5-4-3. It wasn't his first choice because he didn't like to mix business with pleasure. Purp owned the club. Therefore, to him, it was a place of business.

They parked in valet and headed toward the V.I.P. line. As they approached, Huncho took note of the door. Clyde and Tank were working. No one knew of his ties to the Benji Family, so when they stepped in the V.I.P. line and Huncho was addressed, they were thrown off.

"Yo, Huncho, how many you got with ya, baby boy? Y'all c'mon through. Just get ya bands, fam," Clyde said, to Huncho's surprise.

Huncho told him how many were with him and they dapped each other up as he passed through the door to get his V.I.P.. band free of charge. After seeing Huncho visit Purp at the club on numerous occasions, Clyde had inquired as to who he was. Purp had answered with a single word.

"Family."

"Anything you need. Just holla at me!" Clyde said.

"That's what's up." Huncho entered the club with his crew in tow.

It was live.

Half-naked, exotic women were everywhere, pussy-poppin' on stage, giving lap dances, falling off in the "private room." The dance floor was definitely jam-packed. The DJ was crunk and someone had bought the bar, so everyone was feeling good.

"Damn, brah! Who you know to get the royal treatment up in this mu'fucka? The Benji Family owns this shit, don't they Woadie asked.

Huncho smiled. “Come on. Let’s just ball. This my first time out since I been home.”

They entered the V.I.P. area and popped bottles, burned kush, and threw money all night. A few strippers that knew Huncho by name from his visits with Purp came over and acknowledged him, but he kept his business to himself.

While they lounged in V.I.P., he told them about his plans in the game and the position each one of them would play and they all accepted their roles. By time they left the club, everybody was fucked up.

“Damn, what the fuck wrong with that nigga? Shawdy lookin bad as fuck!” Shoota said, watching Pit as he got out of his car in a yellow and blue Akademik ‘fit, stunna shades, and yellow, blue, and black Jordan #13’s.

Shoota and Razor were in the Wayfields parking lot, waiting for Thugga, who was to meet them there to deliver some money. They just so happened to catch sight of Pit at the car wash beside the QuikTrip.

“Shawdy wearing a shit bag now. Nigga got hit in the gut twice ‘bout a month or two ago.” Razor put the final twist on a blunt and put the flame to it to dry it. “He say some niggas tried to rob him, but the nigga ain’t getting no money like that. You know he fuck with them Trigga Mafia niggas.”

Shoota watched Pit head to a change dispenser, stick a couple bills in, and retrieve quarters out of the tray. He took the handful of quarters to a smoker, gave him some instructions, then walked off, conversing with whomever he was conversing with.

“One of Nard’s flunkies, huh?” Shoota was still staring at Pit. “He got them young niggas fooled, don’t he?”

Razor chuckled, “Boi, do he?” He lit the blunt, taking a deep pull. “What Huncho think about the shit the nigga doin’?”

"We talked about it awhile back before he put his face back on the scene and he brushed the shit off, but I could tell he wasn't feelin' it. But brah on some get money shit now and he tryna have shit right for when Dumbway and them come home. They ain't got too much longer before they get out, and you know them niggas like his big homies."

Razor passed him the blunt. "With them niggas being original Mafiosos, I wonder what they think about the nigga starting some shit under the Mafia's name? A mu'fuckin' snitch, at that."

Before Shoota could answer, his phone rung.

"Holla at me, Thug. Where you at?" He talked for a few minutes then ended the call, telling Thugga to hurry up. He and Razor continued talking while they waited. Neither of them knew Pit was watching them from behind the dark shades he wore.

Five minutes later, Thugga and Rock pulled up in a black Chevy Caprice with orange interior. Woadie was in the back seat. They had just dropped ten pounds off in East Point off 29 and were giving Shoota the eight stacks to be delivered to Huncho. They got out of the car, dapped each other up, and kicked shit for a minute. Woadie stayed seated in the car, one foot hanging out, as he sipped a beer. They were listening to a song a Mafioso named Rambo Gotti had recorded the night before.

Rock passed the money to Shoota. "Damn, y'all niggas must've been ridin'. I just got off the phone with you."

"Man, you know that nigga Thugga don't do the speed limit! Nigga be speeding like Clayton County won't stop his ass!"

"Fuck twelve, they can suck my dick. I ain't stopping for them hoes! It ain't like I got license. I ain't got no business in a car no way!" He laughed.

Upon catching sight of Pit talking on the phone, he froze. Shoota and Razor followed his eyes.

He squinted for a better look. "Who that nigga is right there? He look like one of them." He stopped when Pit looked his direction.

Before anything could be said, Thugga was pulling the Ruger from his waistline, cocking it. Woadie sprang into action, jumping from the car, DE in hand. He had shot through an empty stall, going around to cut him off on the other side. Since the car wash parking lot was full, Rock tried to grab Thugga to stop him, but he'd stepped out of arms reach.

***

Pit was on the phone with his brother Mel, telling him the nigga they had tried to rob was at the car wash. He gave his location, trying to keep his back turned but keep an eye on Thugga and his boys at the same time. He knew if he walked back to his car, he would be noticed. Shoota and Razor had already been watching him. He knew they were Southside Mafia, but he didn't know they knew Thugga. Glancing back to make sure he hadn't been noticed, he saw Thugga pull a pistol from his waist and charge in his direction.

"Hurry up, brah! These niggas finna start trippin', shawdy!" Pit's heart was racing a mile a minute.

"I'm right around the corner, bro. Just..." Mel was cut off by the sound of gunshots.

Pit pulled his gun and ran, but the shit bag slowed him down. Bullets flew over his head, whistling by his ears. People screamed and took cover. Others that were washing their cars began to pull off or duck behind their cars as Thugga ran with the Ruger aimed straight ahead, firing off round after round. A bullet hit Pit in the shoulder and he stumbled and dropped his gun, but made no attempt to retrieve it. Bending the corner around the last stall, he headed for Townsend Townhomes. A short distance away, he knew making it there was his best chance at living to see another day.

Woadie came from nowhere, clothes-lining him to the ground. "Where you goin', bitch?"

Thugga came around the corner as he stomped Pit out. After kicking Pit in the face, he pushed Woadie back and shot him five times. Blood soaked the concrete, and in the middle of the puddle, Pit's body laid twitching.

"Fuck nigga!" Thugga kicked him in the stomach for good measure.

"C'mon, let's dip!" Woadie said, dreads half-wrapping his face, left and right, as he looked both ways checking for onlookers.

They ran back to the car.

***

Rock was backing up the Caprice when they came from behind the stalls. Rear door open, Woadie tossed the Desert Eagle in before him and dove in the back seat. Rock was leaning over to open the passenger door for Thugga when a cream colored Expedition turned into the car wash followed by a small gold Toyota with three dread heads muggin'. The high yellow guy in the driver's seat was Mel. Upon seeing Thugga attempting to get in, he swerved to a halt and hopped out, gunning at the Caprice.

Thugga raised the Ruger and let off two shots before it started clicking, chamber stuck cocked to show its emptiness. He tossed the gun in the car and followed it, ducking in the seat as bullets sprayed the windshield. Shoota and Razor had already fled the scene due to them carrying money and drugs, so the three of them were outnumbered. Niggas got out of the Expedition, shooting as Rock backed the Caprice over a curve. He was ducked behind the seat, driving blind.

Woadie stuck the Desert Eagle out the rear window, firing wildly as they bounced into traffic. Cars swerved hard to avoid collision. Rock slammed on the brakes, then snatched the gear into drive, shooting down Flint River Road with Woadie hanging out the window busting shots for cover as they sped away.

Mel found Pit's body behind the car wash as police began to flood the parking lot. He knelt beside him as tears fell from his eyes. His baby brother had died at the age of twenty.

***

Nard received the news about Pit's death and knew he had to retaliate in order to save face with his crew. Mel knew he and Pit were sent to keep Huncho from bubbling in the game, though at the time, both figured it was just another lick he was putting them on. However, when Dru told Nard about Huncho fronting work to Shoota, Rock, Thugga, and Woadie, he figured he could have them robbed. The plan was to set Huncho back, but it backfired, leaving him in a do-or-die circumstance. The only advantage he had was the element of surprise.

Huncho had no idea he was a target.

CHAPTER 4

Dumbway's name was called for mail and he stepped through the crowd of hopeful inmates, awaiting the same blessing. The C.O. handed him two regular white envelopes and one manila. He glanced at the return address of the letters and smiled. Two were from Huncho and one was from his brother Longway.

He walked over to one of the dorm's steel table and sat on it, opening the manila envelope with the pictures first. The first picture he saw was of Huncho, Woadie, Thugga, Rock, and Shoota at Club 5-4-3 with bottles in hand, throwing up the M's. The next one was of them flashing wads of money with multiple strippers posing in thongs and G-strings. The rest were pictures of cars, them just kicking it around the hood, and a couple old pictures of The Spot. That put a smile on his face.

He read his letters next and learned a mild version of Huncho's plans. After reading Huncho's letter, he read the one from Longway. There was an additional letter in it from a Mafioso named Kasaan. They kept in contact by writing through Longway, who forwarded their letters back and forth. He expressed his love for him and the Mafia.

Over and over, he read the letters and went through the pictures. Eventually, he headed to the television room to watch videos with a few of his partnas from the city. Pictures in hand, he found himself flipping through them again with a proud smile on his face.

Mayhem stuck his head in the television room. "Say, Dumbway, They got Clayton County on the news. A nigga done got whacked at the car wash on Tara Boulevard."

He got up and went to where several of his homeboys from Atlanta were gathered, looking up at the television with their arms folded. The reporter was giving details of the shootout and murder of Pit, interviewing witnesses who gave their own account of what happened. Dumbway saw a couple male figures in the background dressed in all black with tip-dyed dreads and knew immediately that they were Mafia. What bothered him was the fact he didn't know either one of them.

"Them niggas going ham out there!" Bloodhound said when the news went to commercial. "Say Way, you know them niggas? They from 'round the way and look like they Mafia."

"Naw, I don't know nan one of them."

Nighttime at hand, he called the number Huncho had put in the letter. The faces from the news concerned him because he didn't know them and was sure they were imposters, from their dreads to their dress code. He had heard of Nard and Trigga Mafia, and planned to deal with the issue upon his release. Huncho hadn't made mention of any new Mafiosos, nor had any of the Frontline that he stayed in contact with. He wondered if they were 8800 or from 7675. He doubted they were 2-DUB.

Huncho accepted the call and it was all love. Dumbway thanked him for the pictures, money order, and for putting money on the phone so he could call him. They did some catching up, and Huncho made a couple three-way calls for him. Before the call ended, Dumbway asked about the incident at the car wash.

"Well, I can't scream no names, but I heard the nigga who got murked tried to rob somebody and they caught up with his ass and gave 'em the business."

"I saw the shit on the news, right, and it was some niggas in the background that looked like Mafia. You know 'em?"

"Naw, brah, never saw 'em before," Huncho said. "But you know that nigga Nard got some niggas under him. They callin' the shit Trigga Mafia."

"Nard! I heard 'bout that snitch-ass nigga. Neither him or them fuck niggas under him is Mafia! Tell the streets I..."

The call ended before he could finish.

***

Huncho got off the phone and finished packing for his trip to Cali. He was headed out west to link up with Ricardo and Carlos to make his first direct purchase from them. The shooting the day before kind of bothered him. He needed his four lieutenants active in the streets. The fifty pounds he was about to cop weren't gonna sell themselves, not to mention the two blocks he'd been sitting on.

He knew Thugga and Woadie would have to lay low for a while, at least until they found out if they'd been fingered for the car wash murder. That left Rock and Shoota, but they would have to do for now. He and Shoota would handle the weed while Rock moved the soft.

Or maybe...

Camry drove him to the Atlanta Hartsfield-Jackson airport and he boarded the plane headed west with five thousand in cash on him. Camry would send the other seventy-five-hundred through Western Union and a cashier's check, along with a couple stacks for spending money. He didn't want to travel with too much because doing so would put him under scrutiny of the IRS. With heightened airport security, there was no way he could risk traveling with that much money in his bags.

His plane landed at LAX and Ricardo was waiting for him by baggage claim. After retrieving his luggage, they exited the terminal and slid off in his white 760 BMW, headed home. Los Angeles was everything Huncho ever dreamed it to be. The beautiful women. The natural beaches. Marijuana galore. The sparkling sky, reflecting off the skyscrapers. As they drove through the City of Angel's, Ricardo pointed out different spots. Some he recognized, others, not quite.

"Weed is damn near legal out here," Ricardo said. "Some people even have license to have it in their possession for medical purposes. We have some of the most exotic cannabis strands in the world. White Widow. Hydro. Blueberry Kush. Orange Kush. Russian Rush. Anything you name, we have!" Reaching in the console, he removed a small bag about the size of a baby's fist and handed it over.

"What's this?" Huncho put the bag to his nose, examining its contents more closely. "Smells like lemons."

Ricardo smiled, turning into a gated community. "Lemon Lime Kush. Comes from Hawaii."

Huncho stared out the window at the multimillion dollar homes that sat nestled in the hills of the city. Cali seemed like another world compared to Riverdale. The manicured lawns. The palm trees. Privacy fences. The opulent mini-mansions were breathtaking.

When Ricardo pulled up to the mansion, Huncho was in a state of disbelief. This was luxury at its finest.

I can see Camry now, Huncho thought, smiling.

Inside, they smoked, poured a couple drinks, and shot pool. Before long, Carlos arrived. Grabbing a beer and pool cue himself, they spent time getting more acquainted, talking little of the business Huncho had come for. After shooting the shit for a few hours, they showed Huncho to the hotel where he would be staying.

The money Huncho was spending was nothing to them. Their interest was in his pedigree as a thoroughbred street nigga with influence. Purp told them how the Mafia was once the most feared gang on the Southside, and they saw opportunity.

If what Purp told them was correct, the money he was spending would more than quadruple in no time.

***

Yummy leaned over from the passenger seat and kissed Shoota on the cheek as they cruised down Highway 85, headed home after a long day of shopping. From Southlake Mall to DTLR. Burlington Coat Factory. Kids Foot Locker. Wal-Mart. They had been all over Clayton County and had the bags on the backseat floor to prove it. Turning back, Yummy entertained their son Jay, making him kick and giggle in his car seat as she tickled his toes.

"Don't you look just like yo' daddy, with yo' handsome self."

Shoota and Yummy had started talking three years ago after he bumped into her and Camry visiting Huncho while he awaited trial for Taliban's murder. What started off as a fling transformed into something worthwhile after Shoota held her down through the loss of her mother. When she ended up pregnant with Jay, there was no looking back. Far from trippin', he chose to man up. Unlike most niggas his age who would've felt trapped, he felt empowered. Their love was an authentic one, and he wanted to give her the world and everything in it, a longing that was now fathomable.

With Huncho's help, he had gone from pushing nicks and dimes to serving pounds overnight. With the greenlight to put other Mafiosos on who had remained loyal from day one, the Mafia was slowly resurrecting.

Upon Huncho's return from Cali, there would be a mandatory meeting, and every set under 2-DUB Mafia would be required to show face.

Even the Queens.

As the sun set, the sky was a purplish orange, and wisps of web-like clouds floated off to nowhere.

"Baby, I'm hungry." Yummy was looking out her window at all the fast food restaurants that lined the strip. "Owww, let's stop and get something to eat while we out."

"What you want?"

"Ummm…stop at Taco Bell."

Shoota sucked his teeth. "Man, hell naw!"

"Baby, whyyy?" Yummy whined.

"'Cause, don't nobody want no damn tacos."

"So! I got a taste for some of they cinnamon twists." Yummy mushed his head playfully. "Come on, bae. Yo' big head self. Fa real! Slow down fo' you pass it."

Shoota tried to bite her hand, but missed. "Do it again. I dare you. I'll bite it off."

Yummy laughed.

Shoota turned his gunmetal Hyundai Genesis into Taco Bell and pulled up to the drive-thru behind a rusty pick-up truck. Tired from the day's events, he laid his head back against the headrest. Reaching his hand under Yummy's sun-dress, he caressed her soft buttercream thigh and closed his eyes as his hand climbed higher and he felt the heat emanating from between her legs.

***

"Aye say, G, ain't that Shoota?" Mel asked, staring towards the drive-thru. He had just walked out of Taco Bell with two take-out bags, and was now standing outside the driver's side door of Mel's Expedition.

Gino let his seat up and followed his gaze, squinting his eyes. "Shiiid, damn sho' is, shawdy." He pulled a black .40 Cal from under the seat. "What's up?"

"Naw, this nigga mine." Mel pulled a .380 from his waist and cocked it. He looked around the fairly empty parking lot. "Just pull across the street and wait on me."

Mel got out of the car with the pistol down by his side as Gino pulled away. Walking normally, he held his head down so his dreads concealed his face, but kept his eyes on Shoota's car. No one seemed to notice him as he crept toward the car with the gun. He could hear his own heart beating in his chest with every step he took.

Three more steps and it's a wrap, he thought.

Eyes trained on Shoota, he moved with stealth, finger wrapped around the trigger, ready to squeeze. Closer now, he raised it to the window.

"Hey, Mel!" a female called out, distracting him for a split second.

***

Shoota was laid back, massaging Yummy's close-shaved pussy through her sheer lace thong, when he caught movement in his peripheral vision. He turned to look, and found himself staring headlong down the barrel of gun.

"This for my brother Pit, fuck nigga!"

BWA! BWA! BWA!

Blood and brain matter splattered all over Yummy, who was screaming at the top of her lungs, as Shoota lay slumped over the console, head leaking in her lap. Mel stuck his arm through the shattered window and fired two more rounds in his side before taking flight. The girl that had been calling his name had ducked out of sight at the sound of the first gunshot.

***

Gun in hand, Mel dipped and dodged traffic across 85, as he shot toward the Spin Cycle parking lot, where Gino sat ready with the door open. He hopped in and they sped off as witnesses looked on in shock.

***

Yummy got out of the car screaming and crying, her shirt and face covered in blood. In the back seat, Jay was crying his eyes out as if he understood that something had gone terribly wrong. She snatched open the back door and tried with trembling hands to unclasp him from his car seat, but her nerves were shot. She was hysterical. Giving up, she stumbled back from the car, mumbling and sobbing incoherently. Without a doubt, she knew that Shoota was dead. She ran her hands back through her hair, trying to make sense of what just happened.

"Ma'am, are you okay?" An elderly man approached slowly. "Help is on the way."

That was the last thing Yummy heard before she collapsed in the parking lot from blood loss. She had been so out of it she hadn't realized she'd been shot in the arm.

***

"Acompaar el alla yo querer ser ahi en uno hora hacia cumplir officio." Carlos was telling Ricardo to escort someone to a meeting spot and that he would be there in an hour to do business.

"Percabir t aht luego," Ricardo replied, saying he would see him there, then turned, facing Huncho. "That was Carlos. We have to make a stop before we go to the spot I was telling you about."

Huncho nodded, lounging in the seat of the Lamborghini Murcielago Coupe. The gas they'd been smoking all day had Huncho higher than a murder bond. Before the call from Carlos, they had been on their way out to do some sightseeing. Ricardo was going to take him through some of the hoods that were infamous, made famous by rappers and movies like *Menace to Society* and *Boys N the Hood.*

He had told Huncho of his cartel connections and how when it came to getting money, the only color that mattered was green. Huncho accepted his philosophy and began telling him about the Mafia.

Halfway to the ranch outside Los Angeles, Huncho peeped a tail. They were being followed by a black F-350 with tinted windows. When he pointed them out to Ricardo, he smiled, telling him they were good. At the ranch, they turned in behind them. Huncho still hadn't seen who drove the truck. All he knew was that they spoke Spanish from the conversation Ricardo held with them over the phone. They exited their vehicles and Huncho took a deep breath, taking in the fresh air blowing over the ranch. He stretched, sneaking a peek at the occupants of the truck that followed them to the ranch, and saw that it was three clean cut Migos. They gave him a head up nod, and he returned the gesture.

They entered the house and were escorted out back to the patio, where Carlos was standing looking out into the distance with his phone to his ear, speaking in rapid Spanish with a glass of bourbon in his other hand. They all took a seat and one of the Migos set a large duffle bag on the floor next to him. Carlos brought the phone conversation to an end and turned to face his company.

"Acogida amigos hacia m casa hasta cumplir officio." Carlos welcomed the Migos to his home to do business, then turned to Huncho. "No offense, they only speak Spanish. Bear with us for a minute. Would you like something to drink?"

"Yeah, anything cold'll do," Huncho said.

Carlos yelled something in Spanish toward the patio door and seconds later, an older Spanish woman appeared with Coronas on a tray, offering one to each of the visitors.

He sat and listened as Carlos and Ricardo spoke back and forth with the Migos for about twenty minutes until their leader lifted the bag from the floor and placed it on the table in front of Carlos. He unzipped the bag and pulled out two wads of money that were rubber-banded on each end. He thumbed the end of one, holding it to his ear with a smile before saying something in Spanish that made them all laugh. Carlos nodded his head, and the bag was taken in the house by the same guy that escorted them to the patio. Twenty minutes later he reappeared, nodding his head once. Carlos returned the gesture, said a few words, then they all stood in unison, shaking hands with a smile. Huncho stood as well, sensing the meeting had come to a happy ending.

Ricardo motioned with his head for Huncho to follow. They walked back through the patio entrance and out the front door. The first thing that Huncho noticed was the bales of hay on the black F-350. Carlos shook hands with the Migos again before they headed out to the truck. Huncho knew without a doubt that more than hay had been loaded on the back of the truck. He, Ricardo, and Carlos returned in the house and had shots of tequila. Having just sold forty bricks of cocaine, they toasted to the money. After refilling their glasses, they made a toast to Huncho.

Ricardo held his drink in the air. "To the start of great business dealings!"

"To great business dealings!" Carlos and Huncho said in union. Clinging glasses, they downed another shot.

"So Huncho, how do you like the west coast so far?" Carlos asked.

"It's a'ight," he said. "I just gotta get Ricardo to slow down so I can enjoy the scenery."

Ricardo laughed. "You think that was fast. I hadn't been driving half as fast as I usually would. I had to slow down so the vatos behind me could keep up."

Carlos put his hand on Huncho shoulder. "You might want to say a prayer before the ride back." He laughed. "You couldn't pay me to get in that damn thing with him. No fuckin' way!"

"I got a better idea." Ricardo held out his keys. "How 'bout you drive back?"

Huncho stared at the keys for a second, then smiled, nodding his head. "Now that's what I'm talkin' 'bout."

When they pulled away from the ranch, Huncho was behind the wheel blasting "Stunt" by Gucci Mane from the speakers. Having smoked another blunt before they left, they were feeling good. By the time they reached Highway 5, Huncho had become accustomed to the exotic beast. On the highway, he pushed it to the limit, reaching nearly 170 MPH before letting off the gas. The adrenaline rush he got was something he'd never experienced before. He knew right then and there he wanted his own.

He turned into the parking lot of the hotel he was staying at. "Man, I gotta get one of these mu'fuckas!"

"You know, when you buy one, you can build it and pick out what you want inside and out. They have the best I've ever seen," Ricardo said. "Six months after you buy it, you can sell it back to the dealer. And if you want another one, you can just pay the difference for the new one. You can even pre-order it. You can't find a better deal nowhere else. That's why I fuck with them. I'm on my third one."

As Huncho pulled up in front of the hotel, his phone began to ring. He looked at the screen, saw it was Camry, and answered immediately. “What’s up, sweetheart?”

Camry was crying hysterically. “They killed him, Daldrick!”

“What! Who, baby?”

“Shoota! They shot him in the head,” Camry cried, sniveling. “Yummy, too. I’m on my way to the hospital now. Oh my God! Daldrick, Jay was in the backseat!”

Huncho had one foot out the car with the door raised, but couldn’t force his body to move. He was numb. Ricardo sensed something was wrong from the change in his demeanor, but said nothing.

“A’ight, let me call you back when I get inside. Stay by the phone.” Huncho hung up.

“Everything alright?” Ricardo asked.

Huncho stared off at nothing. “One of my boys…he’s dead.”

***

Two days after Shoota’s murder, Huncho was back in Riverdale after cutting his stay in Cali short by a few days. His package had arrived at the spots he mailed them to, and everything went as planned. But with the tragedy that had befallen Shoota, he was unable to focus on business. Shoota’s murder was clearly retribution. Yummy said the gunman had yelled something about the hit being for his brother Pit. If this was true, that meant his entire crew was in danger. He needed to find out who was responsible, so he called the mandatory meeting earlier than he had planned and set the new movement off right with the introduction of the new spot, a two-story house off Scott Road.

In The Spot's not-yet-furnished living room, Queens were everywhere, dreads with dyed tips were prominent amongst Mafiosos, and gray bandannas hung visibly from the necks, wrists, and pockets of 2-DUB affiliates. Huncho noticed their increase in numbers. Either that, or he had never known how deep they were from the jump. He spotted Woadie posted in the back corner of the living room beside Longway, sporting a black "Free CT" shirt, some blue jeans, and a pair of all-white One's.

Hollywood, Razor, Pee-Wee, and Fresh walked in the front door, all Mafia except Hollywood, something Huncho knew only because of the "Second To None" shirt he wore. After he closed the door behind them, they went and sat on the stairs, choosing to stay to themselves.

Huncho got the meeting underway, letting it be known how the Mafia was rocking and what would be expected of all affiliates.

After giving each crew ten pounds to sell, the Mafia was officially going in for the takeover. 7675 Mafiosos would work Riverdale and Forest Park. 8800 Block Mafiosos would work Morrow and the Rex Road area of Ellenwood. And 2-DUB would work Lovejoy, Jonesboro, and the Clayton County area of Stockbridge. Out of respect for the peace treaty with Hit Squad Taliban, they would refrain from setting up shop in the 4900 area of College Park. Although the Dirt Gang movement in Morrow - or Jurassic Park, as it was referred to by its natives - had the capacity to pose a threat regarding territory issues, the Mafia was moving in anyways. After all, they had put the South on the map.

Huncho broke a block down between the sets that moved in areas where coke would bump the fastest, then gave one to Rock to cook up and re-up the Mafiosos that would need it. At the meeting's end, he made his final announcement.

"I want the head of the one responsible for murkin' Shoota." Sweeping his gaze back and forth over the crowd, Huncho locked eyes with each individual in the room. "The streets talk. Keep your eyes and ears open."

Putting the Mafia in position to get money solidified his influence. With the blessing of the entire Frontline, he knew they would follow him to the end. 2-DUB was all the same. Wrong or right, they were riding.

***

Huncho rushed home to pick Camry up and take her to a new restaurant on Peachtree Road that served Moroccan food. Because the restaurant had an intimate setting, they dropped Zakayla off with Huncho's mother. Tonight was their night, one they were determined to enjoy.

They arrived at their location, heading inside, where they were immediately serviced. Hand in hand, they fed each other while reclining on satin pillows in a dining room-like atmosphere, entertained by Moroccan belly dancers. It was something new to the both of them, and Camry was surprised at the change in Huncho.

It was as if the money was maturing him. To Huncho, it was something else altogether though. It was the beginning of a lifestyle he had envisioned while lying in a cell. It was his mission to ball for every nigga who would never see the streets. For the ones that even if they did get out, their life would still be over due to spending their best years as an inmate.

He knew what it felt like to go to bed every night thinking he might never see the streets again. He had been blessed with a second chance and with the life he had been given back, he was going to live it to the fullest.

They rode back home listening to soft R&B.

"Start looking for us a house," Huncho said. "I want us to be movin' within the next month."

Camry looked at him, lost for words. She reached over and took his hand in hers. "Okay."

The remainder of the ride was done in silence. His mind was on the money to come. He knew Shoota's killer would be found and dealt with in no time without him raising a finger. And once this first package was gone and the Mafia was getting money as an organization, he could sit back, chill, and put the next part of his plan in motion.

The next morning he awoke early and took the hour and forty-five minute drive to Trion, Georgia, a mountainous area in North Georgia located just before the Tennessee border. Pulling into the Hays State Prison parking lot, he cut the engine and sat for a minute, staring at the prison as visitors made their way to the facility's entrance. Taking a deep breath, he got out and did the same. After signing in and being searched, he was admitted in and five minutes later, D-Day was coming through the door with a smile as bright as the morning sun. It had been over two years since they'd seen each other.

They embraced.

It was all love.

CHAPTER 5

Nard was laid back with his hands locked behind his head, looking down at the exotic beauty stroking his shaft as she licked and sucked his balls, staring up at him. They had been going at it for the better part of the night. She was on X and he was high on cocaine. She smiled, teasing his manhood with the tip of her tongue, before taking it to the back of her throat. After sucking him nice and slow, she pulled him out her mouth, jacking him with vigor.

"Come on, put it back in your mouth." His voice was almost a whisper. He grabbed a handful of her weave, guiding her head back to his lap. "Yeah. Just like that. Suck that mu'fucka, baby."

She played with his nuts, massaging his scrotum with her tender fingers. There were deep grooves in her cheeks from the suction as her head bobbed in a rhythmic motion.

Ever since Nard started getting money, he had been fucking some of the baddest bitches in the metropolitan region. It was as if they could literally smell the money on him. No matter where he went, he was bound to bag a broad, bedding her within a week's time.

Having always been a playa, money only amplified his status. Before, he was fucking tennis shoe bitches. Now his roster consisted of the high maintenance type. Christian Louboutin. Emperio Armani. Michael Kors. Christian Dior.

Della was half-black, half-Dominican, with long curly brown hair, sexy pouty lips, a slender nose with a diamond stud, arched eyebrows, ass and tits out this world, yet miraculously slender. A junior at Spelman, she majored in Computer Information Systems and minored in Marketing. She was striving to be a Software Developer. Nard paid her tuition and bought her a car to get around. He met her at the Georgia

Dome during the Battle of the Bands Festival and they'd been seeing each other ever since. Money was originally her motive, until she fell in love with the sex. She was an undercover freak and so was Nard.

He bent her over on all fours, spread her knees wide, put a deep arch in her back, and fucked her like a dog until he exploded inside her. They collapsed on the bed, out of breath. When his breathing somewhat steadied, he slapped her on the ass and told her to go get him something to drink. Reaching on top his nightstand, he grabbed a box of Newport's, withdrew a single, and fired it up, taking a deep pull before exhaling a thick cloud of smoke.

Della stepped back in the room with a bottle of Grey Goose, a bowl of ice, and some cranberry juice they had been sipping. Nard was just setting the bag of coke back down after snorting a two-on-two off a car key.

"My own personal Tony Montana," she said, stroking his ego. "Just don't overdo it. I'm not through with you yet, papi," she added, knowing too much coke sometimes kept him from getting an erection. She wanted more than her pussy eaten tonight.

She fixed them both drinks and put in a flick that led to more fucking. After another session, they laid atop the covers, exhausted. Nard's phone was ringing, but he couldn't hear it. He was dead to the world. After sleeping late, they finally got up and he took her home and got back on the grind for the money he had missed out on the day before.

After dropping her off, he checked his voicemail. The first three messages were from TMC Skeet, telling him to call ASAP, stressing the seriousness of the issue. After going through the remaining voicemails, deleting unimportant messages, he returned his call. As it rang, he wondered what could be so major that everyone was blowing his phone up while he tried to get his freak on.

"Nard!"

"Yeah, what's up, li'l homie?"

"Mel, brah. He got a warrant on him for a body. They kicked in his door last night."

Nard wasn't sure he'd heard him right. "What?"

"It's all bad, big brah. They done been by his mama's and his baby mama's crib," Skeet said. "My bitch say Clayton County was deep as fuck."

"Where he at now?"

"Shiiid, don't nobody know! That's why I'm callin' you, just in case you happen to run across him. Tell him to get the fuck outta dodge. 12 still over in Greystone, so he can't be out there nowhere. Damn. I can't even go pick my bitch up."

Nard already knew what was going on. Mel had called directly after fleeing the scene. He was the one who put him up in a condo. For three weeks, Mel called his mother to see if the police had been by looking for him. Nothing. He watched the news coverage of the murder. His name was not mentioned. Hearing nothing about being wanted, Mel chose to come out of hiding.

"Find out where he is and tell him I said hit my line, ASAP. If he needs anything, get it for him and put the word out for everyone else to do the same."

"A'ight, brah!" Skeet said.

They ended the call.

***

Thugga and Woadie had been laying low for over a month in Newnan, Georgia. Both were ready to come out of hiding and get back to the money. Huncho made sure they had everything they needed, even females. He wanted them comfortable so they would stay put. But even that wasn't enough to make them want to stay after hearing about how the Mafia was getting to the money. Now they wanted to find the one who had killed Shoota.

They were sitting on the sofa in the living room of the house they had been set up in in East Highland, playing Fight Night on Xbox 360.

"I don't know how much more of this shit I can take, brah!" Woadie lit a Newport. "I'm tired of this Coweta County-ass shit!"

"I been tired of this bullshit," Thugga said. "It ain't like 12 ridin' 'round with our pictures, screamin' a nigga name, feel me?"

"That's what I was tryna tell Huncho, but he still on that we need to chill and lay low bullshit. I ain't finna keep sittin' down here in these mu'fuckin' woods like this!"

Thugga hopped up. "I'm tryna tell ya. Them niggas out there getting money. Shiiid, I wanna ball too!"

Woadie sat silently, pondering the whole situation.

2-DUB and Southside Mafia were seeing more money than ever. Huncho had reunited the original Mafia to stand alongside the second generation of Mafiosos and taken them to another level. He had been back to Cali and copped another fifty pounds of popcorn and twenty pounds of Blueberry Kush. For every five bricks he copped from Purp, an additional five were fronted. The Mafia had nearly taken over the Southside, squeezing money from every trap and corner they could. They were hitting the club sometimes fifty and sixty deep, pulling up in tour buses, leaving the crowd to wonder if B.M.F. had resurrected. All the while, Huncho's two most valued gun slangers watched from the sidelines.

Woadie stood up from the sofa. "Man, fuck this shit! I'm out. I'd rather take my chances in the streets!"

"Shiiid, let's ride then, my nigga. I'm wit' ya!" Thugga agreed without hesitation.

Woadie dialed a number into his phone and brought it to his ear.

***

Shanika was a twenty-two-year-old beauty and mother of a one-year-old. To make ends meet, she danced four days a week at a club called The Brazilian. She didn't plan to make it a career. She was only doing what she had to do to pay her way through school and have enough money to support her and her daughter.

Fairly short, she had long hair that she wore straight, letting it flirt with the top of her chest. Her eyes, innocent and doe-like, added to her stage seduction by selling you the fantasy of the proverbial temptress. She had ass and tits for days and her skin was a blemish-free earth tone. She had been offered several free photo shoots to start a modeling career, but having her mind focused on school, she turned down all offers and continued dancing, her mind set on a business degree. Her roommate, Crystal, helped her with her daughter when she was working or attending classes and had become somewhat of a surrogate mother in her absence. Not that she didn't care for her. She was just trying to secure a future for her daughter.

For the last couple of weeks, Shanika had been at home more than usual, only going to her classes. She was avoiding the club, afraid she might run into Mel. He might want to question her about what she had seen at Taco Bell that day. Or worst, he might kill her too.

She had been questioned at the murder scene after another witness implicated her, saying she had called the killer seconds before he started shooting. So therefore she was left with no other option but to cooperate with the detectives and tell what she had seen and knew about the shooter.

But there wasn't much she could tell about him. She only knew him from being in the club. She didn't know his government name or where he laid his head. All she knew was that he came to the club on the regular, spent a lot of money, and had given her his phone number, which she did not tell the detectives. But surveillance camera footage from the Taco Bell parking lot led the authorities straight to Mel's identification, and when she saw his mugshot from a previous arrest on the evening news, she got scared and feared for her safety, thinking she was the reason Mel was wanted for murder.

"Man, I need some money!" She was sitting Indian style on her bed, holding a Sprite. "I need my nails and shit done and I'm tired of wearing that hot-ass fucking wig!"

Crystal sat on the edge of her bed, doing her niece's hair with a blunt between her fingers. "Why don't you go back to work? I doubt that the nigga be out at a strip club knowing he has a warrant for a body with his face on the news."

"He don't have to be. He in a gang, I think. Every time he come to The Brazilian, he be with a bunch of niggas with dreads and they always talking about some shit called Trigga Mafia."

"Trigga Mafia?" Crystal said. "That's them niggas that's tryna be like my cousin's clique. The nigga that run the Trigga Mafia used to be in the Southside Mafia 'til he snitched a couple years ago."

"Southside Mafia?" Shanika wore a quizzical expression. Since she wasn't connected to the streets, she knew very little about them.

"That's my cousin's crew. They got the Southside sewed up. You seen them before. Probably seen them in the club. Just didn't know who they was, and- " Crystal stopped mid-sentence, hands frozen in her niece's hair. "Wait. You say he be with them Trigga Mafia niggas?"

Shanika nodded, taking another sip of her Sprite. "What? Why you lookin' like that?"

"Because the nigga he killed is from the original Mafia. They lookin for his ass right now. You ever heard of Huncho?"

Shanika shook her head. "Uh-uh."

"What! You ain't never heard of Southside Mafia! Huncho the one got everybody on. They say he the one got money on Mel head for killing Shoota. They was tight."

"Why doesn't he just kill Mel himself if he's so powerful?" Shanika asked.

"He just beat a murder on appeal." Crystal hit her blunt, exhaling as she greased her niece's scalp. "He callin' shots, he just rockin' low-key."

Crystal went on until Shanika received a phone call. She took the call, went to her room, and laid across her bed, staring at the ceiling as she talked to the guy she had been dating for the last six months. Downstairs, Crystal was on the phone with her cousin, telling him about Mel's TMC affiliation.

***

Camry had just returned from doing some much-needed shopping for their new home, after a long day at school. It was a split-level four bedroom with a double garage and a lake in the backyard that sat in the middle of the low-key subdivision in College Park known as Thornton Woods. Every day since moving in, she had gone out to buy something new for the house. She had her own computer/study room, which she had made look like a home office. Huncho spent most of his time in the basement, so much so that the rest of the house was basically hers.

She pulled into the garage just as Huncho was about to hop in his Escalade. He stopped at his driver side door, waiting for her to get out. Zakayla was asleep in the backseat. Camry got out of the car, still in her school scrubs and he walked to the other side to meet her.

She was noticeably tired.

He hugged her and she wrapped her arms around his waist. "You grab the rest of the bags out the car so I can get Zakayla and take her in."

"Yeah, I got you. You straight?" He kissed her soft lips.

"Umm, for the most part, I guess."

Huncho shook his head. "Pleeease, you look sleepy as fuck."

"A little tired. Zakayla showed her ass on me. I had to carry her and the bags 'cause she wouldn't walk."

Huncho chuckled. "Naw, she ain't do you like that."

"Uhhh, yes. She did."

Huncho laughed this time. "Girl, go lay down. I got you."

"Thank you, baby." She gave him a peck on the lips. "When you get back, I need you to put this table together I bought for the patio."

He carried the bags and table from the trunk.

Once finished, he hopped in his new Escalade and backed out of the driveway. Purchased a week ago, it still had that new car smell. Even better, there were less than three hundred miles on the dash.

The day after buying it, he put some Ashanti rims on the wheels and took pictures standing next to it and squatting by the 26's with ten bands spread out like a fan. All hundred dollar bills. He sent the pictures with two hundred dollar money orders to D-Day, Dumbway, and a few other Mafiosos behind the wall.

The smell of the new truck made him feel good as he cruised along Old National Highway, listening to a song by a young nigga from Riverdale named Dreak. A real problem child, he was somewhat seasoned, but had never done a crime he hadn't had to do. He simply wanted more for his girl and grandmother and felt that sometimes you had to do the wrong thing to make shit right.

Huncho discovered Dreak at The Bleu Room, a home studio on Grove Street where most local jokers got their start. Dreak had just turned seventeen and was trying to finagle his way onto the rap scene with a swag that made Huncho wonder how anyone in their right mind hadn't signed him yet. He was the truth.

Huncho found him advanced for his age. Book and street smart. Just what he needed. The face of an authentic street label.

He called TD and it was on.

Break Free Records was back!

One night after a session, he pulled Dreak aside. After learning he was from Pine Hill, where he had grown up with his grandmother, he offered him a spot in the Mafia. He bucked. He tried to give him ten stacks. Bucked.

They dapped up.

No hard feelings.

Huncho continued pulling up, searching for raw new talent, but none measured up to Dreak in comparison.

Three months later, taking note of Dreak's absence, he questioned Slim, who told him Dreak had caught a case. Two months prior, he'd been arrested for Theft by Receiving Motor

Vehicle.

Thinking Suge Knight, he set out on a mission. He found out his grandmother's apartment number, priced out his bond, and had a Queen drop off the money with a number to call once he got settled.

Two weeks later, Huncho was pulling up on him with a contract for fifteen thousand. He was straight on the Mafia, but he accepted the Break Free Record contract, making it clear the money hadn't been what swayed him. Asked what he meant, he said the gesture had done it.

"Niggas ain't keepin' it real like that no more," he said. "Whatever you with, I'm with it."

Huncho nodded, knowing he had made the right choice, snatching him up. Dreak was the most solid young nigga he had come across since he beat his appeal.

He made a vow to himself that day to do everything in his power to insure Dreak's success. Not just that, but to personally see to it that he actually make it. He was in the process of building a studio in his basement, determined to succeed where, only three years ago, the Mafia had failed.

He turned off S.R 138 onto Scott Road, pulling into the driveway of a white and burgundy house. The new spot. Hopping out, he made his way inside to find an unexpected surprise in the living room.

"Shawdy! What the fuck is y'all doin' here?" Thugga was on the floor on his stomach, looking up at the television, mashing controller buttons furiously. Woadie was sitting on the cream love seat, a lit blunt hanging loosely from his lips. Pistols laid within arm's reach, on the coffee table. They cut their eyes at him and continued playing Madden.

"Shawdy, what's up?" Huncho waved his arm to get their attention. "Y'all niggas trippin'!"

"Maaan, we ain't 'bout to keep sittin' down that mu'fucka. Y'all trippin'," Woadie mumbled, hitting the blunt, its tip glowing a hot red. "That shit ain't puttin' no money in our pockets."

"You ain't gon' have to worry 'bout no money sittin' in Clayton County with a mu'fuckin' life sentence if these crackas catch you and bam yo' ass out!" Huncho was heated.

"Maaan, them folks ain't e'en studdin' us." Thugga looked up at Huncho. "They ain't been to our spot or nothin', brah! It's been over two months. The streets ain't talkin'."

Rock walked in from the kitchen, a surgical mask lifted to his forehead. He had been in the kitchen cooking up coke when he overheard the heated exchange. Taking in Huncho's mug, he shook his head and gave Thugga and Woadie an I-told-you-so face.

"Holla at me when you through in here." He pulled the surgical mask over his nose and mouth. "Oh, and, uhhh… you're wasting your time with them two." He headed back into the kitchen.

Ten minutes of reasoning got nowhere fast. Having done his best, Huncho gave up and headed to the kitchen. Rock was at the stove, sprinkling water in a Pyrex pot with a mixture of coke and baking soda. On the counter were baking soda boxes, forks and spoons, a line of glass beakers, and several pieces of crack the shape of a beaker bottom. Huncho lifted a large piece of crack the size of half a beaker, examining it.

"How long you been at it?" he asked.

Rock raised the pot from the stove. "Shiiid, a couple hours. I done did half a brick and some extra shit I had layin' around."

"What's up with them two in there?" Huncho asked, throwing his head towards the living room.

"That's Hard Head and Head Hard," Rock said. "That's what I call 'em, anyways."

"It damn sho' fit 'em." Huncho set the crack back on the counter. "What's up, though? You wanted to holla at me?"

"Crystal called."

"Crystaaaal?"

"My cousin, Crystal," Rock said. "Tony's sister. Remember?"

"Tony? I don't kn - Shiiid, hold on." Huncho nodded. "Cuz fuck with the yams. Yeah. Brah put me and Flame on some licks out in Griffin. Stayed in, what - Spaulding Heights?" Huncho's brow furrowed as the memory surfed into a tidal wave. The only females he recalled at Tony's spot were the jump-offs he and Flame brought through. "He shook his head. "I don't think I know shawdy."

"Probably not. She cut him off when she found out he was using." Placing the pot back on the stove, Rock grabbed a fork. "Anyways, the nigga that shot Shoota...his name's Mel."

Huncho folded his arms. "How she know?"

"Her roommate saw the whole thing, recognized him from The Brazilian." Rock worked his wrist, scraping the pot, whipping the water clockwise. "The nigga Thugga and Woadie murked at the car wash: Pit, Mel's baby brother. And get this, both brothers run with TMC. Well, minus Pit."

Huncho nodded, pondering what Rock said. "Think Nard's bitch ass got somethin' to do with this?"

"I know he do! This shit wit' Pit and Mel, too." Rock fanned the pot with a piece of cardboard. "The nigga paranoid! He so shook you might expose him, he ego trippin' on the strength. I say we pop!"

Huncho shook his head. "Wars make it hard to eat. That what you want?"

"What I want is some paper! But I ain't feelin' the shit I been hearin' lately." Rock threw the cardboard on the counter, growing serious. "They shot up one of our traps in Forest Park. Emory got ran off the block in Hunter's Ridge. Fuck that. We the real Block Boiz! What's up? Let's show 'em."

In that moment, Huncho realized why he favored Rock. He was another Flame. His reasoning. His persona. That fire burning inside, threatening to break free. That selflessness. He was always his brother's keeper. You never had to question his loyalty. If he fucked with you, he fucked with you. If not, it was fuck you. It was what it was. Whatever you was on, without a doubt, he was with it.

I miss you, my nigga, he thought, dropping his head in sorrow. *Damn, shawdy.*

Huncho pondered Rock and Flame's character similarities. It was obvious that Rock had idolized him to a great magnitude. That was clear. Even clearer were the qualities he seemed to value in people, the morals and codes he singled out, voluntarily choosing to adhere to. That said a lot. The fact that he was seventeen said even more. With the right guidance, he could be great. He himself was evidence of this. In four years he had gone from being just another young'un to Riverdale's finest. Rock could too. He would help him develop. Mirror his drive. Breed him for greatness. Just as he had for Dreak, he vowed to see to it that they have a chance.

The one Flame never had...

Nard was number one on the Mafia's shit list. Not only was he a rat, he had emulated their image, misleading the streets into believing they were an official 2-DUB Mafia set. Left unchecked, they had free reign to run renegade, and their membership spread. Huncho looked up. Rock was right. It was time to take back their respect. End the shenanigans, and let it be known that the streets still belonged to them.

The real Mafia.

Huncho took in Rock's stance. Feet firm. Shoulder's squared. Head high. He was a real one. "Show 'em, huh?"

"Damn right!"

Huncho nodded. "Let's push the button on that shit, then."

CHAPTER 6

Mel had been kicking it with Maria, his latest side piece, when he received word that he was wanted for murder. Paranoid from having his face on the local news, he ducked off in Morrow in Cobblestone Apartments and later retired to The Drury Inn for the night.

His life had spiraled downhill since his brother's death. He was trying to pull things together, but couldn't seem to focus. Too many thoughts. Too many emotions. He was suffocating. It felt as though the entire world was closing in on him, and fast. He needed a way to come out of this unscathed.

After sending Maria out for Chinese food, he hopped in the shower. The feeling of the hot water cascading over his head and body was relaxing, therapeutic even. Listening to the artificial sound of pelting rain, he racked his brain, hell-bent on a solution. Over and over, his mind replayed different scenarios, running through all the possible outcomes.

He cut the shower off, wrapped a towel around his waist, and walked into the room to find Maria naked in the center of the bed, stroking her clit seductively.

Letting the towel fall from around his waist, he climbed on the bed and mounted her.

The unmistakable sounds of blissful sex filled the hotel room, faint tones audible in the hall by those in passing. Tempting melodies to the ears of lovers. Sweet music to those committed.

Mel held Maria's legs back by her ankles, unleashing his frustrations on her tight pussy. Sweat dripped from his body onto the creamy skin of her petite frame as he sexed her like crazy. With each clap of flesh meeting flesh her head, cushioned by her disheveled bun, banged against the headboard.

Mel released Maria's ankles, rested them on his shoulders, and leaned forward, palms on either side of her, to stroke deeper.

"Get this pussy!" Maria cried. "Sí, papi! Sí! Fuck it like it's yours." Her bun was coming undone, releasing strands of long black hair into her face. She tossed her head and whipped them free. "Sí! Sí! Sí! Ah, Yes! Work that big dick, baby!"

Mel caught Maria's legs in the crook of his arms, hitting it harder as he raced toward climax. She bit her bottom lip, taking the dick like a big girl. Pressure building, he plunged in, deeper still.

He came just as the door crashed in, sending wood fragments flying to the floor. The door smashed into the wall and armed S.W.A.T. officers flooded the room in full tactical gear.

"Clayton County PD!"

Mel lunged for his .380 on the bedside nightstand, slipping out of the pussy with a wet pop. Maria screamed, snatching the sheet to cover her nakedness.

"Freeze!" The officers rushed the bed with infrared beams spotting his body. "Don't fuckin' move!"

Mel laid still on his stomach, hand hovering above the nightstand, just inches away from his gun. Behind him, Maria was still screaming. He mumbled a curse under his breath, wishing he could grab his strap. A few seconds' heads up would've made all the difference. He could've gunned his way out of the hotel, using Maria as a human shield.

"On the ground! Now!" Officers circled the room, surrounding him. "Put your goddamn hands on your head. Now, motherfucker!"

Jaws clenched, Mel raised both hands to the back of his head, staring at Maria's pedicured toes as she was escorted out of the room wrapped in a sheet.

Shoving a knee to Mel's back, the lead officer pulled a pair of handcuffs from his waist and placed them on Mel's wrists, never mind the fact he was completely naked. He stood, pulled the sweat drenched blanket off the bed, and used it to cover him. Giving two officers the order to "Take him away," he watched as Mel was flanked, hoisted from the floor by his arms, and hauled off.

Outside was a circus. Law enforcement vehicles filled the small, dimly-lit parking lot. Camera crews and reporters set up for segments. Riverdale and Clayton County PD officers roamed about, policing the area.

Bystanders crowded the sidewalk, watching in awe. This was the closest to meeting a killer they had ever been, or would ever come.

The cool night air caressed Mel's face as he descended the stairs. He glanced at a window and the curtain zipped shut. So much for innocent until proven guilty. The little Indian man who owned the hotel peeked from his office window at a safe distance. He was probably the one who had called the folks.

"Scary-ass Navaho," Mel said to himself.

After loading him into the back of a paddy wagon they slammed the door, leaving him feeling numb.

***

Ace was Nard's favorite. He was known for the fat sacks of powder he sold up and down 11 Stackz, but his post was the Southside Inn Hotel on Tara Boulevard.

Where he was now…

He had been Trigga Mafia for a little over a year and like the true hustler he was, he'd been stacking paper ever since. Nard kept him supplied with clean coke. He never ran out. His clientele list was extensive.

He was 'bout his bread.

On any given club night, you could find him in the trap. He didn't care much for flexin'. He was more concerned with seeing his check go up. It was all work, no play with him.

Ace had the discipline of a monk. He had been known to bust down bricks and dub them out, one half at a time. The very reason Nard kept him with the best.

Some nights he had too much money in the room. So much so, it made him paranoid. Suspicious of all plays, he would close shop, load the Draco, and sit on the bed, facing the door, swearing he heard a pistol cock right outside.

Tonight wasn't one of those nights, but his phone was beatin'. It had been ringing every five minutes for the past hour. He served a play at the Hooters down the street and caught another one for a four-way just as he made it back to the hotel. A set of high beams eased up behind him as he crossed the lot, headed back to his room.

Thugga crept through in a stolen Dodge Ram, Bang-Bang riding shotgun.

Coming up on him, Bang-Bang flagged him down. "Say, brah, you know where I can get some soft?"

Ace spun around and lifted his hand to shield his eyes from the headlights."

"I ain't 12 or nothin'. I'm just tryna get on it."

Ace eyed the idling truck with suspicion. Convinced that Bang-Bang wasn't the folks, he pointed to an empty parking space. "Pull in right here. I gotcha."

Ace approached as Thugga backed into the parking space, stopping at what he presumed to be a safe distance. "What you tryna get?"

Bang-Bang whipped out a fat wad of cash. "Shiiid, 'bout two or three grams if the ticket right."

"I'll fuck with you for thirty since you gettin three of 'em." Ace pulled a sandwich bag from the front of his pants, glancing around the parking lot.

"Don't I know you?" Bang-Bang asked in surprise. "You fuck with TMC. Ace, right?"

Ace tried to get a better look at Bang-Bang. "Yeah, I'm Trigga M- "

Woadie shot straight up in the bed of the truck with two Desert Eagles aimed at Ace's face. "2-DUB!"

Ace dropped the bag of dope and attempted to run, but it was useless. He hadn't taken three steps when the .45 hollow points coming from the Desert Eagle twisted his body, lifting his body off his feet.

"Gottem Gang or no name, nigga!" Bang-Bang stuck his .357 out the window and put two in the back of his head.

Thugga peeled off, burning rubber.

***

Camry decided to visit Remede', a Buckhead massage parlor in St. Regis, for ninety minutes of premium pampering. She had become accustomed to the high life and felt entitled to a stress-free day. So when made aware of today's forty dollar special - a pedicure consisting of a soak and scrub, followed up with a lotion massage - she couldn't resist treating herself. The feeling was so relaxing, she nearly fell asleep.

Feet done, she underwent a Cosmopolitan, which included an aesthetic scrubbing of her hands with a gritty scrubber, an enzyme peel moisturizing massage, and some time inside the sauna that smelled of mints. She stepped out with a towel wrapped around her head, feeling rejuvenated, skin tingling from the mint vapors.

Inside her car, the first thing she did was call Huncho. They spoke briefly, making plans to go out that evening. Camry hung up, anxious to see what Huncho had in store for the night. It had been a couple weeks since they last met. It would be the perfect setting to reveal the secret she had been holding.

She pulled out of the parking lot, dialing her mother's number to tell her about Remede' and check on Zakayla. Unbeknownst to her, she was being followed. In fact, she had been followed since dropping Zakayla off that morning.

***

Nard and Della were sipping Pinot Noir over a plate of spaghetti tossed with raw shrimp, scallions, and sausages at La Pietra Cucina, an Italian restaurant he'd been turned on to by one of his side pieces.

It was a celebration. Having successfully completed 120 semester hours and received her credits as a full-time student, she had been awarded her Bachelors of Science in Computer Information Systems.

Nard was proud of her, and even more so of himself. Three years ago, he had come home an exile. He had been run off the Southside by his former Mafiosos and relocated to the eastside, where he met his plug.

She was his first legal investment. Nevertheless, Della and her career were second on his mind.

Ace had been killed a few nights ago and two of his spots had been robbed. He knew 2DM were behind it, and that Huncho was calling the shots. He hated himself for giving Huncho time to reunite the old Mafia and get his money right. He was becoming a thorn in his side. He hadn't thought Huncho could reunite the Mafia as quickly as he had. Underestimating him had cost him dearly.

"Did you hear what I said?" Della asked, snapping him from his thoughts.

"I'm sorry, baby. What were you was sayin?" Nard pulled a napkin from the table dispenser. "My mind had drifted to my li'l homie's funeral that's coming up."

Della reiterated her job choices, but again, Nard was only half listening. He was waiting on a call from Dru and Gino. Sensing his attention elsewhere, she enjoyed her food and wine, deciding to discuss her career another time.

Later that night, they sexed each other like never before, collapsing after climax in a breathless heap of exhaustion. Nard held Della in his arms as she drifted off into a peaceful slumber. Unable to sleep, he eased out of bed and headed downstairs to boot up on coke. He had just snorted his third line when his phone rang. He licked his finger, swiped up the fourth, and stuck it in his mouth, swishing his finger around.

"What's the word?" he answered on the fifth ring.

"It's done," Dru said. "The package is secure."

Nard swallowed a drain and cleared his throat. "Pull up at the destination. I gotta handle something before I swing through."

He hung up, bumped a pile of coke from the end of his truck key, and went upstairs to wake Della so he could take her home.

***

Huncho was at Patchwerk Studios with, Dreak, a tall, young nigga with a dirty brown skin tone. He had good hair, chest length dreads, a stout but cut build, and a budding goatee.

Dreak was nearing the end of a four-hour block session. The studio was owned by former Atlanta Falcons player Bob Whitfield. Huncho had been turned onto the studio during a conversation with Purp, who frequented the establishment. Nearly all high-profile artist from Atlanta had recorded or got their music mastered there.

Prominent artists came through and Huncho gave nothing more than head nods in passing. They were on their grind, just like him. He was the star-struck fan of no one. His idols were authentic street niggas, not some fake-ass studio gangstas who had never stepped foot in a trap or busted their guns. They were lucky he was getting money now. Three years ago, there would've been a tragedy.

"You can come out for a minute," Dez said into the mic. Dreak could hear him through his headphones inside the booth. "I'ma clean this last verse up then let you do your adlibs."

Dreak stepped out of the booth, all smiles. Huncho passed him a bottle of water, nodding his head with satisfaction, before turning back to watch Dez track out Dreak's vocals.

During each session, he always paid close attention to the engineers and producers that he worked with to learn all he could about the production side of the business. So far, he knew what programs to use and what equipment to purchase for his own studio that he planned to build in the near future.

Purp and 3-Co, a Benji Family rapper, came through for a session in a separate studio room. Huncho stepped aside to the smoking area to have a few words with Purp in private. Shortly afterwards, Huncho and Dreak left the building.

He dropped Dreak off and called Camry to let her know he was on his way home, only to get her voicemail. He left her a message.

The conversation he and Purp had was still fresh on his mind. The Feds were at Roscoe, one of Purp's main men, meaning more than likely, they were really at him. That would change the way they had been operating. Understanding the chances he was taking by dealing with Purp, he continued.

To risk nothing in life was to risk everything.

***

Huncho pulled into his garage, tapping the wireless responder clipped to his sun visor, closing it shut behind him. Taking note of the empty space beside his car, he checked the time on his phone. He got out and headed to the kitchen, calling Camry to see where she was, but got her voicemail. He retrieved a glass of apple juice from the fridge, trying her number, only to get her voicemail again. He sipped his juice, waiting for the beep, deciding to leave another message. He even sent a text.

Another hour went by and she still hadn't returned his calls. Figuring she might be at her mother's house with Zakayla and just had her phone off, he decided to go by her parents' house.

Twenty minutes later, he was turning into King's Manor, noticing immediately that Camry's car was nowhere in sight. He drove into the driveway, got out of his Escalade, and knocked. Moments later, Camry's mother opened the door, surprised to see him on her doorstep.

"How're you doin', Mrs. Watkins?"

"Oh, I'm fine, Daldrick. Is everything okay? You're not here for Zakayla, are you? Camry said she would be staying until tomorrow."

Huncho was starting to get a bad vibe. "Well, actually I, um... You talked to Camry?"

"Not since she dropped Kayla off this morning. Why, is something wrong?"

"I've been callin' her all day and she hasn't been returning my calls."

"Hmm, that's strange. Let me get my phone and see if I can get ahold of her."

She invited him in while she went to get her phone. She closed the door behind him and he waited in the living room. Mrs. Watkins returned, holding a cordless phone to her ear. A moment passed and she brought it down with a worried expression.

"She didn't answer my call, either. That's not like her." She sat in her La-Z-Boy chair. "I'll keep trying, but it's probably nothing. Don't overreact. Zakayla's in there on my bed asleep if you wanna see her, though."

"Naw, it's cool. Let her sleep. I'ma head back to the house in case she tries to call there. If you hear from her, have her call me."

Mrs. Watkins walked him to the door and watched as he backed out the driveway and pulled off.

Back at home, Camry's car was still absent from the garage, and she had yet to call. The longer he waited, the angrier he became. He rolled a blunt and fired it up to calm himself down. Halfway through, his phone rang. Seeing Camry's number, he answered.

"Where the fuck you been?" he raged, hopping up from the sofa. "And what the fuck wrong with yo' phone that you can't answer that mu'fucka?"

"You through with the Captain-Save-A-Hoe shit, nigga?" a male voice said.

"What?" Huncho looked at his phone like it had just licked his face. "Who the fuck is this?"

"I'm the nigga that need a hunnid bands if you ever wanna see this bitch alive again. So I advise you to empty yo' piggy bank and get to countin', nigga."

Huncho couldn't believe what he was hearing.

"Oh, and any sign of 12, they'll find this bitch in pieces."

Click!

"Hello!" Huncho yelled. "Hello!"

The caller had hung up.

Huncho cursed the air and slung his phone into the sofa. Camry had been kidnapped, and was being held for a hundred-thousand-dollar ransom.

CHAPTER 7

Mel sat in The County in 4-5. His charges consisted of Murder, two counts of Aggravated Assault, Possession of a Firearm during the Commission of a Crime, and several other minor offenses. According to detectives, he had been identified by a stripper that knew him from The Brazilian, earning his face a feature in a photo lineup, where several other witnesses confirmed him as the shooter. As far as trial, his chances were slim to none. He was no fool. Beating the case hadn't been on his mind. He was banking on a bond so he could get out and skip town.

Nard offered money for his attorney fees, but he told him to hold it until he got a bond. Why waste money on a lawyer to fight a case he knew he couldn't beat, when he could use it to slide? His bond was bound to be a hundred thousand or more. He needed every penny he could salvage.

Each day he worked the phone, calling everyone he could think of to see what they had to offer. He had a little over ten thousand dollars of his own money stashed away, and he told his people to put a for sale sign on his Expedition and box Chevy. He sold his watch, his bulletproof vest, and a couple guns over the phone. Refusing to have money put on his books for commissary, he chose to live off the land. Every dollar counted, and he wasn't about to waste it on zoom-zooms and wam-wams.

"Say, shawdy, you'll make a call for me? I'll shoot you somethin' for fuckin' with me," another county inmate asked. He had been trying to reach out to his people for a few days. Seeing Mel dial a number on the phone, he pulled up to try his luck. "It won't take but a minute. I just wanna tell my baby mama to come see me and put some money on the phone so I can call."

Mel looked over his shoulder to find it was Retro, the guy who slept next door to him that was always arguing on the phone. "Shiiid, what you talkin 'bout shootin' me?" As the call went through, he bounced his leg rapidly.

"I got you two items," Retro said. "What you want? Soups? Racks? Or Icy's?"

Mel thought for a moment. "I tell you what, I'll let you get two whole calls for a Colgate and a Sure deodorant."

"Shiiid, hell yeah. I can't give it to you 'til they pop our cells, though."

Mel held up a finger as the call was accepted. He said a few words, passed the receiver to Retro, and moved two phones down. His girl had three burnout lines that he used to gain commissary items. He dialed another number and talked until rotation ended. They had to lockdown for shift change.

He got his toothpaste and deodorant from Retro and went in his cell where his bunkmate, a slim cat with a li'l twist from 138 named Brando was looking out a hole in their window at the visitation parking lot.

"Them hoes out there lookin' good as fuck, shawdy," he said in a daze. "These crackas gotta let me up out this mu'fucka, fa'real, shawdy. Look at that bitch right there with the capris. Bet money she comin' to see a lame or put money on his books. If I was out there, I'd pull up on that hoe blowin' that loud, sittin on 6's with them Yay's on and it'd be a wrap for whoever it is she comin' to see."

Mel hopped on the top bunk and looked out the hole in his window as he laid on his stomach. He had to admit, the female was lookin' sexy, even from how far up he was. Nevertheless, he was far from moved by her physique. His mind was on walking out of the County and never returning.

"You know somebody that might wanna buy a box Chevy?" Mel asked for the sake of conversation. He had already deduced Brando to be a compulsive liar who flexed about what he had and did.

"Shiiid, I can holla at my folks. I know they'll snatch it up from you. That's all they fuck with is them Chevy's and shit. They got that work, too. You never heard of Vito?" Brando asked, making Mel hate that he ever asked the question. "Shawdy be whippin' a bloody red Charger on them 4's with the five percent tint."

"Naw, brah, I don't know him, shawdy."

"But shiiid, I'll hit him up next rotation. He should have some money on the phone for me," he lied. "What you tryna get for it, though?"

"It's a 1970, been skeeted down, pearl white with some 4's on it. Tan interior, beat and five TV's in it. That bitch runnin', too. I gotta get at least ten bands for it. That's the least I'll take for it. I spent damn near that on the rims."

They continued talking about cars, Brando dominating the conversation with his jail cell lies. The topic took many turns, but when it got to Southside and Trigga Mafia, Brando switched to listening. Mel spoke highly of Nard. How he was up. How he had put Lovejoy on. How he was 'bout his issue. Nard being from his hood, Brando knew Nard to be a snitch, but didn't expose him. He just listened, asking questions when necessary.

The convo lead to gunplay, and who was out there really puttin' on for that South. Brando knew Mel was locked up for murder, but hadn't known the details. Hearing him talk about how he had killed Shoota in retaliation for the death of his little brother, he was shocked at how freely he spoke of crossing the Mafia.

"You ever heard of a nigga named Huncho from Riverdale?" Mel asked. "He Southside Mafia. Murked Taliban four years ago at the Sparkle's and beat the murder case on appeal."

Huncho was also from his hood. They never hung out, but they spoke in passing. Brando decided to play his hands close to the vest to see what he could find out.

"I heard of him, but I don't know him like that. What about him, though?"

Nard got a ticket on his head," he said. "And he don't e'en know it."

***

Camry had been held captive for two days. Since then, she remained locked in an unfurnished room with cream-painted walls on the second floor of a house. She knew she was upstairs from looking out the window. The room she occupied was on the back side of the house, facing some woods. Out of curiosity, she had tried to lift the window, knowing even if she did get it open, there was still nowhere to go. The window was too high to jump, and even if it wasn't, she still had to deal with the menacing-looking pit bull in the backyard. Needless to say, she abandoned the window as an escape route.

How had she ended up in this situation?

She tried to replay the kidnapping in her mind, but it was hard. It all seemed so…foggy.

All she remembered was being rear ended at a stop sign. When she got out to assess the damage, she was grabbed from behind and forced into the trunk of her car at gunpoint by four masked men. A wet cloth was pressed to her nose and mouth, and everything went black. It all happened so fast she didn't even get a chance to see what kind of car they were driving.

The ski masks they wore made it impossible to identify them, not to mention her being blindfolded before taken out the trunk. She took that as a good sign, though. Bare-face kidnappings usually meant the perpetrators didn't intend to let their victims live, something she'd heard so long ago, she couldn't remember where from. She had no idea where she was. All she knew was that wherever they were, it required a long ride on the expressway.

More than once, she had been put on the phone so Huncho could hear her voice. Of course, they didn't get to talk. He heard her crying, and she would hear him yell "hello" just before the phone was snatched away. The kidnappers then demanded money, ending the call without so much as another syllable. Well aware of the blood on Huncho's hands, she hoped that was all this was about.

Her eyes were swollen from crying and she had been refusing to eat the food the kidnappers brought her. Whenever she heard one of them at the door, she would lay in a fetal position, playing possum until they left the room. She said a silent prayer as she thought about Zakayla.

The door opened and she closed her eyes, playing sleep. As one of the kidnappers approached, she peeked, but he was wearing a ski mask. Her body was weak from lack of food and dehydration, making it easy to lay still. She readied herself for the unthinkable, feeling his presence looming over her.

He nudged her shoulder with his foot. "Aye...aye!"

Camry opened her eyes as if waking for the first time that morning.

"Put ya shoes on. We goin' for a ride."

"Where are we going?" she asked wearily.

"For a ride," he snapped. "Now put your shoes on and let's roll. I ain't got all day."

Afraid to anger him any further, Camry did as she was told. Bound and blindfolded, she was led outside and placed in a vehicle that smelled of heavy weed smoke. Knowing it was a car and not a truck, she was reminded of how one sense worked better when another had been disabled. Her hearing and sense of touch had heightened, but when the car started and the music came on, she was lost once again. All she could hear was music and mumbling up front.

***

Huncho sat, phone in hand, in the passenger seat of a rented Chrysler 300, a hundred thou in a duffle on the floor between his legs. Behind the wheel was Rock, and on the other side of the parking lot Woadie, Thugga, Thump, and Fatt sat in a tan Honda Civic, watching the scene through binoculars. Huncho had been instructed to go to Southlake Mall and wait for further instructions. He had been clearly warned that if a single police showed up, Camry would be killed.

No police had been contacted. However, there was a Mafioso at every entry and exit of the mall.

Due to Purp being out of town, it had taken a day and a half to come up with the money. Once able to get ahold of him and explain the situation, he hadn't hesitated to provide the twenty thousand dollars needed to complete the ransom demand. At the time, Huncho had only been able to scrape up 80k.

He could've sold the bricks he had for cheap, but that would've taken time. So he chose to get it from Purp instead, giving him his word that he would take care of him on the back end once he got off the work.

With no idea who was behind the kidnapping, he was keeping it esoteric. Save for a trusted few, no one knew Camry was missing. He had even talked the kidnappers into letting her call her mother to make sure she didn't get the police involved, thus insuring Camry's safety.

Huncho took a sip from a can of Crunk Juice and placed it back in the cup holder in the middle by the console. He hadn't slept in the two days she'd been gone and it showed in his bloodshot eyes. Yet he stayed alert, refusing to let them shut.

His phone rang, startling him. He answered on the second ring.

"You have a collect call from..." An array of background conversations filled the pause. "An inmate at the Clayton County Detention Center."

It was an automated Secures' operator. Someone was calling him from the county jail. Curious as to who or what could have transpired, he accepted the call.

"Whaddup, shawdy!" The voice was unfamiliar.

"Who this?"

"It's ya boy...Brando!" He seemed excited, an emotion Huncho was starting to forget existed.

"Brando? Brando, who?"

"From the hood, brah!" Brando took off, talking a mile a minute.

"Aye, aye, brah. Brando…Brando." He shook his head, growing irritated. "Aye, Brando man, goddamn! Shut the fuck up! Shit!"

"Oh, my bad, man. What's up?"

"Hit me back a li'l later. I'm in the middle of something impor…"

"Wait! wait! wait! Hold up!" Brando said. "I got something you might wanna hear."

Huncho paused, thinking of Camry and the kidnappers. “Say...how’d you get my number, anyway?”

“My cousin Duck shot it to me.”

“Who?”

“Duck. Got the trap in Emerald Point. Be shoppin’ with you on the bags.”

Huncho knew exactly who he was talking about. Duck was one of the few people he served directly.

Maybe he knows something, Huncho thought. “I’m listening.”

“A’ight, so my cellmate, right. Some TMC nigga named Mel. Shawdy talkin’ real reckless. Say he clapped Shoota and Nard, got you walkin’ on ice. So really, I’m on some shit like - “

“A’ight, brah, ‘preciate that info. Hit me later, though.”

“Hold up, one m-”

Huncho hung up before Brando could speak another word. Knowing all County calls were monitored and recorded, he refused to talk or react on the phone. Not about no shit like that.

He dropped his phone into his lap and stared out across the busy parking lot, pondering what he just heard. Brando was known for flexin’. The Frontstreet motto was “believe nothing Brando said, and half of what he showed you.”

Yet his words coincided with what Crystal told Rock. Though Nard had every reason to be behind this, Huncho hadn’t been so quick to label him as Camry’s kidnapper. They were at war, true enough, but success had many enemies.

His phone rang again, this time the call he’d been waiting for. He answered on the third ring.

“You got what I want?”

“Been had it. You the one late.”

“You where I told you to be?”

Huncho sucked his teeth. "What you think?"

"Answer the mu'fuckin' question!"

Huncho gritted his teeth. "Everything good on my end. What about you? Let me hear that she's okay. I wanna know that you ain't bullshittin'. Show me you a man of yo' word."

"Just make sho' that paperwork straight!" the kidnapper snapped, authority present in his tone. "That's all you need to worry 'bout right now."

Rock was watching Huncho, hanging from his every word. He was on the phone with Thugga and Woadie, giving them a play-by-play as they followed the action from their post.

"Naw, brah, this money means nothin' to me. I need to know my baby's a'ight before we go any farther."

There was a moment of silence before Huncho realized the caller had clicked off the line. He was about to hang up when he heard ringing in his ear. The kidnapper was making a three-way call. Camry was put on the phone for a brief second to confirm her safety. Then the third party disconnected, leaving the original caller to instruct Huncho to the drop spot.

Huncho gave directions and Rock drove through the parking lot, aware, yet unconcerned, that he was being watched. No matter where they went in the parking lot, someone from the Mafia could see them.

Southlake Mall was poppin', and the lot was full of comers and goers. Females of the finest quality. Young niggas exiting with shoe bags galore, two of which reminded him of the weekends he and Flame had spent ripping and running through Southlake.

He shook it off.

As instructed, he pulled into a parking space four slots down from a tinted Nissan Altima with paper tags in place of the license plate. He got out with the phone pressed to his ear, dropped the duffle with the money next to it, and turned to walk off. Halfway back to the Chrysler, the passenger door of the Nissan flew open, an arm snatched the bag in, and the car peeled off.

"What kind of game you playin', brah?" Huncho yelled into the receiver. "Where my girl at?"

"Man, hold yo' mu'fuckin'; horses, shawdy. The money's being checked. If everything good like you say, you'll get what you came for."

Huncho and Rock rode around aimlessly, scanning the parking lot for anything that stood out.

Thugga and Woadie had already got a tail on the Nissan. It was their job to keep track of the money. The Nissan circled the parking lot, apparently to make sure they weren't being followed. Satisfied that this wasn't the case, they exited the lot, flying down Mt. Zion Boulevard.

"Go to the main entrance parking lot," the kidnapper instructed. "You'll see a blue Buick Century. Pop the trunk from the inside."

Then the line went dead.

Rock shot through the parking lot as Huncho got ready for whatever. Before the car came to a complete stop, he was already hopping out. Pulling a black 9mm from his waist, he held it down at his side as he ran toward the Buick. As he approached the car, he noticed it was still running, and at the driver side, he saw the steering column had been peeled. Using his shirt to open the door, he reached inside and hit the yellow button, popping the trunk.

He ran to the car's rear, lifting the trunk to find Camry in a fetal position, bound, gagged, and blindfolded. Rock had stopped the car, leaving it running in the middle of the aisle.

Together, they lifted her from the trunk as people stopped and watched.

The Nissan had been followed to a house off Buffington Road in Union City. Woadie, Thugga, and two members of 2-DUB named Thump and Fatt parked down the street and cut through a neighbor's backyard until they were at the house.

Circling the perimeter, they peeked through windows, casing the inside to better formulate a strategic ambush.

A slight crack in the curtain of a side window showed the team of kidnappers dumping the money on the coffee table, celebrating the spoils of what appeared to be another successful lick.

The identity of the kidnappers exposed at last, they were filled with rage and disbelief.

Taking note that the front door opened up to the living room, they made their way to the front of the house.

Wasting no time, Woadie kicked the door in, Desert Eagles in hand blazing. His accomplices were right behind him, firing shots, aimed at the chest up. The perpetrators were in the living room recounting the money, and had no time to react under the hail of gunfire. The smoke cleared, and Thugga put a bullet in each one of their heads to make sure they were dead.

"Get the money and let's dip!" Woadie said.

On the way back to Riverdale, Thugga called Huncho to let him know they were in route with the money.

"Who the fuck them niggas was?" Huncho said.

"Brah, you ain't gone believe this shit," Thugga said. "It was Hollywood, Fresh, and Pee-Wee."

"Da fuck!" Huncho was enraged. "Ain't no mu'fuckin' way! The same niggas I been breakin' bread with!" He was so mad he hung up on Thugga.

Huncho and Rock rode on in silence.

Having heard the unilateral conversation, Rock wondered who within the team had played the game so treacherously, but saw fit to leave Huncho to his thoughts.

Huncho couldn't believe it. His own people. He was no stranger to betrayal, but this kind was of the greatest magnitude.

Another Judas remained within the clique. The perpetrators who had rode off with the money had been killed. This snake had orchestrated the whole play. The one who had done the talking. The only one from that circle of affiliates that wasn't named to be dead in the house off Buffington Road.

He remembered them attending the meeting at The Spot, showing up together, posting up on the stairs. He knew exactly who he was. The kidnapper he had been talking to was still living.

On borrowed time...

CHAPTER 8

Exploited by his very own, it became clear to Huncho that money had no friends. The hood was quick to scream money changed people, but nobody talks about how it changes the people around you. No one was to be fully trusted - not even his own crew. Camry had to change her routine so she wouldn't be vulnerable to such attacks. He was trying to figure out a way to relocate his mother so she wouldn't be targeted, but most of all, he wanted Nard and the last kidnapper dead, who was none other than Razor. He had been brought to the Mafia by Shoota after the car wash murder.

Camry began to complain about him hustling. She would argue and fuss about him being out late, and keeping money in the house, finding ways to put their daughter in it some kind of way.

"What if Zakayla would've been with me, Huncho?" or "What if they come again and take our baby this time?"

"They're not comin' back, so stop worrying about it!" he would say.

But nothing he said was ever good enough for her.

Some nights she went to her mother's house to stay when he wasn't home. Huncho would return, infuriated to discover an empty house. Most of the time it ended in a shouting match over the phone, with one of them hanging up on the other and cutting their phone off.

Things had changed within the Mafia as well. The Spot was no longer a spot to just chill. It was a place strictly for business. No longer did Huncho pull up to the club fifty and sixty deep. His entourage now consisted of a select few, certified street soldiers like Thugga, Woadie, Rock, and Bang-Bang.

The only person he trusted outside that circle was Dreak.

Huncho took Camry to a Chinese restaurant. He figured it was time for them to go on a much-needed vacation and he planned to break the news to her over dinner. The night before they had been arguing because he hadn't come in when he said he would. He was fed up with the fighting, and understood that most of it stemmed from stress.

The waiter served them spare ribs with clay pot cooked Taro roots, but they sent them back after tasting them, replacing them with Tilapia, sautéed tofu, and garlic-flavored chicken. Settling for the fish and chicken, they talked.

"We need a break from all this BS." Huncho sliced off a piece of tilapia, stuck it in his mouth, and chewed. "What d'ya say we take a li'l vacation?"

"Yeah, I think that would be nice." Camry hadn't looked up from her plate. "Besides, in a few months I won't be able to travel anywhere."

Huncho paused mid-bite, looking at her questionably. "Why you say that?" He started back chewing.

Camry's eyes began to water, and Huncho stopped chewing, asking her what was wrong.

"I'm pregnant," she said. "I was going to tell you the night they kidnapped me. I'm, well, a little over twelve weeks."

Huncho was lost for words. No wonder she had been so fussy lately. He reached over the table, taking her hands into his own. Camry's heart raced, unsure of his next words, but upon seeing his smile, she couldn't help but show her very own.

"It better be a boy this time," he said.

He got up, went around the table, and took her into his arms, squeezing her tight with joy.

Camry giggled. "Daldrick, stop, you're hurting the baby."

"Oh, my bad." He laughed, giving her a quick kiss.

For the rest of the night they sat side by side, feeding each other their meals.

They left the restaurant hand in hand. On the way home, Huncho told her about the trip he planned for them to go to Vegas.

Two weeks later, they were flying first class to Sin City.

***

Mel posted the one-hundred-fifty thousand dollar bond and left the County with no intentions of returning. Ever. Not having to run at the moment, he had time to get his money up. But by his next court date, he planned to be on the other side of the map.

He had only been out a few days and was lurking due to him spending and selling everything he had. After all the money pitched in to get him out, his pride wouldn't allow him to ask for a handout, so he was back to living off the land.

Nard had been telling him he was going to put him back on, but he wasn't getting money like he used to. Not since the Mafia had stepped back on the scene and took over his traps. Every penny Nard made he had to get out and grind for it himself, whereas he used to have workers he fronted work to. Money was so short now that he couldn't afford to pay workers or front the ones he did. He had resorted to breaking down bricks.

Another unsuccessful day faded to darkness, and as night settled, Mel found himself in the passenger seat of Nard's Range Rover. They were on 11 Stacks, parked on the side of the road in Greystone.

"I got you, brah. I'm just waitin' on my folks to get back in town so I can fuck with you how I want to, feel me?" Nard said. "The li'l shit I got now already sold. So I'm fucked up 'til then."

Mel listened intently as he relit the blunt. He could feel he was being lied to, but was unsure why. Feeling that Mel was on the verge of snapping, Nard did what he did best. He manipulated the situation.

"Look, my nigga, I'ma be straight up with you. Now you know I ain't never lied to you. We been folks since day one. When you called me for that li'l bread, I ain't bullshit you like the rest of these niggas out here. I even offered to get you a mouthpiece to represent you."

Mel looked down at the blunt in his hand, nodding in agreement, thinking of those who had abandoned him in his time of desperate need. Seeing the affect his words were having, Nard drove his point home, going in for the kill.

"I dropped ya girl twenty bands to get you up out that mu'fucka, 'cause you a real nigga and I know you would do the same for me." Nard declined the blunt, shaking his head with a wave of his hand. "Listen though, brah. This the straight drop truth. No cut. Something I ain't told nobody." He paused for a second, letting his words sink in. "I'm fucked up, Mel. That nigga Huncho got my dick in the dirt. He damn near givin' the dope away out here."

Mel exhaled a cloud of smoke. "I thought he only fucked with the weed?"

"Yeah, when you left. Now he fuckin' with the coke, and he makin' it hard for us to eat out here in these streets." Nard released an exasperated breath. "From the looks of it, the only way we gon' get it out here is if he gone. Real talk. I got fifty bands to make it happen."

The sound of fifty thousand was music to Mel's ears. He would've done it for much less, but for fifty thou, he would do it ASAP with no problem. Nard cranked the car and they rode out talking, Nard telling Mel of the many different spots Huncho frequented, along with other intel he had come across as well. Knowing Mel never intended on showing for court, it seemed as though he was doing him a favor. Having agreed to take the contract, Nard took him to The Brazil.

***

Razor was regretting the decision he made to kidnap Camry. He still hadn't figured out how the others had ended up dead so quick. He had watched Huncho and Rock leave the mall parking lot and followed them until they got on the expressway. But when he pulled up to the rendezvous spot off Buffington Road where they were to meet and split the money, he had to bust a U-turn because the street was blocked off with yellow tape and the house was a triple homicide murder scene.

With his three cohorts dead, he knew he had to go into hiding.

He had been friends with Shoota for years. The day Thugga and Woadie murked Pit at the car wash, Shoota offered him a spot in the Mafia. So he got down, and began seeing more money than ever. The more he saw, the more he wanted. He began feeling he wasn't getting his just dues, and that there was favoritism toward certain Mafiosos. He also took Huncho as soft because of his laidback demeanor. In his eyes, he was hiding behind the Mafia.

One night while rolling on Ecstasy with Hollywood, Fresh, and Pee-Wee, Huncho came up and the truth came out about how he felt. At first the other three listened in silence, but the more he talked, the more sense he started to make. One by one they began to voice their opinions and feelings about how Huncho was running the Mafia until the subject came up about robbing him, but they knew that would be risky. More than likely they would have to kill him, and neither of them were killers.

Thus, the kidnapping was planned.

Running for his life, he now wished they had just gone ahead and killed him.

He did have one ace in the hole, however. A trump card that could very well save his life.

There were a lot of people who wanted Huncho out of the way. People who stood a strong chance at pulling it off. People who could make it happen with the right information.

He checked the time on his phone and headed out to Lovejoy to the female's crib he had been staying with in Tara Glenn.

He had to find Nard.

***

Shanika had been back dancing at The Brazilian since word of Mel's arrest reached her. The time off had done her more good than bad. She had caught up on her rest and picked up a few pounds she had lost from all the late nights working and fast food eating. Not to mention the fact that her customers missed her.

She wore her usually long straight hair in kinky curls. Blemish-free as ever, the earth tone hue of her skin looked even more alluring, body oiled up and sprinkled with glitter, giving her the appearance of a walking jewel. With curves that complemented her juicy assets, she was one of the most popular dancers in the club, not only because of her physical attractiveness alone, but also for the down to earth attitude she extended to the customers. There had been many nights she got paid and hadn't even had to dance. She had tricks who gave her money just to sit and talk.

Her name was called for her to take the stage and she did so in a sexy black and gold negligee, wearing black patent leather thigh high boots. Multi-colored lights danced over the surface of her skin as she stole the hearts of all men present. At the beginning of the fourth and final song, she went to the edge of the stage and got on her hands and knees, making her cheeks jump one at a time. She looked over her shoulder to watch herself work it, but locked eyes with Mel instead.

Her ass stopped, eyes growing wide with fear and disbelief. Mel's stare sent chills up her spine, leaving her flesh covered in goosebumps. Alarmed, she got up and ran to the back as fast as her boots would allow, tripping as she neared the back. The crowd she was entertaining began to boo, and surprisingly calm, Mel slowly walked away from the stage, telling Nard he was ready to go.

Had he not been on a mission for fifty stacks, he would wait outside the club and follow her home, but just because she would live to see another sunrise didn't mean her day wasn't coming.

Shanika ran to the dressing room and called for security, crying and shaking as she explained what happened. While two security guards canvassed the crowd and club looking for Mel, another stood guard at the dressing rooms entrance as she got dressed and cleaned out her locker.

After gathering her things, she was escorted out to her car by two security guards and a Clayton County police officer. She checked her rearview all the way home, paranoid that she was being followed.

That night she made up her mind that dancing was a pastime for her. She was relocating.

***

Bang-Bang and Rock pulled away from a rim shop on Tara Boulevard. It was mid-day, and Rock had just left his 1972 Cutlass Supreme to have a new set of rims put on it. The paint job was pearl blue. It had a white convertible top and 350 V8 engine under the hood. He had a golden burl wood grain finish, sand color ostrich leather interior by Ashanti, and twenty-two inch D'Vinchi rims wrapped in Pirelli tires that completed the car.

They were whipping the same Dodge Ram that had been hijacked the night Ace was murked. It had been repainted a glittery navy blue. The tags had also been switched, replaced with a legitimate license plate. Rock got a girl he met at a Hillandale party to apply for them. Come to find out, she stayed at a group home down the street. Through her he met Kush, a gutta bitch from College Park, who plugged him in with some Arabs at a chop shop in Marietta. Having had the VIN numbers on the car parts swapped, the truck was as legal as twenty one.

It was now Bang-Bang's.

They were cruising down Tara Boulevard when Bang-Bang decided to stop by the Metro PCS store to pay his bill. After swerving into the small plaza, he hopped out in a white wife beater, skin as black as a stoner's lips, a grey bandanna hanging from the front right pocket of his blue jeans. His cocaine white One's were the only thing fresher than his Boosie fade. He opened the door and got stuck holding it open as two shapely females - one chocolate, the other a rich honey skin complexion - walked out, all smiles.

Rock looked on from the passenger seat of the truck, talking on the phone, while he waited for Bang-Bang to handle his business. He shook his head, cracking a smile as Bang-Bang started chumping them off after they refused to give him their number. Then he went inside.

Everyone knew Bang-Bang was slick throwed off. That was no secret. Originally from Red Oak Projects, he had the legal right to be. His older brother Juice was an original member of the Lightning Boys, a Red Oak gang that terrorized the College Park area in the late 90's early 2000's. He was gunned down in front of Bang-Bang by the police, but not before teaching him the art of living by the gun. After relocating to Riverdale when he was twelve, he grew up in Pine Hill to be a trigger-happy Gottem Gang official.

He was 2-DUB to death. In fact, he wasn't feeling the 2DM movement. He fucked with Southside Mafia and all that, but in his mind, it was Dub or die. At eighteen, he was older than Rock, but you would never know if no one told you.

Rock was ahead of his time. He was a thinker, a go hard one at that. Anyone with eyes could see that he had taken Shoota's place as Huncho's right hand.

He was a born leader.

Rock continued to work his phone, conversing with plays, when he spotted Nard and some Dominican chick getting in a Range Rover parked out front of Zaxby's. He looked in the Metro PCS store to see if Bang-Bang was being serviced yet.

"Look, shawdy, I'ma hit you back, a'ight?" Rock was staring at Bang-Bang, willing him to the car with his mind. "Yeah, I mean - yeah. You know what I mean. A'ight, a'ight, cool. You already slow."

Rock hung up, glanced back at the Zaxby's parking lot, and saw the Range Rover pull off down Tara Boulevard.

"Shit!" Quickly, he speed dialed Bang-Bang, simultaneously throwing the truck in reverse. He could've gone and got him out the store, but didn't want to lose sight of the Range Rover. He climbed over into the driver seat as the phone rang.

"Yeah, man, I'm almost done," Bang-Bang answered.

"Brah, you gotta handle that some other time. Nard just pulled off from the Zaxby's. C'mon!" Rock cranked the truck and pulled to the mouth of the lot, straining to see which way Nard had gone, taking note of the unusually light mid-day traffic on Tara. He spotted Nard, fifth car from the red light a little ways up.

Bang-Bang snatched the door open and hopped in the passenger seat. Burning rubber, they peeled out the parking lot in pursuit of Nard.

"Look like he 'bout to turn. I'ma slide up on him, and put him to yo' right. Fye his bitch ass up!" Rock said.

Bang-Bang was mugged up, teeth biting hard into his bottom lip. He held his .357 down between his legs, rolling his window down. "I'm 'bout to let this fuck nigga have it."

Bang-Bang put his hand on the dash for support as Rock weaved in and out of lanes, whipping the truck like a NASCAR driver. Up ahead, the traffic light turned yellow just as Nard made a right onto Mt. Zion Boulevard.

It turned red, and Rock ran it to ensure he didn't get away. The Range Rover was in the middle lane.

Rock flushed the Ram, swerving and dipping through traffic.

"Gottem!" Bang-Bang stuck his arm out the window and let loose.

The driver side window shattered and fell inside, held together by the tint. The truck swerved right as Bang-Bang emptied the clip into its side, and Rock stepped on it, taking a side street behind J-Paul's back to Tara.

After side-swiping a station wagon, the Range Rover barreled headlong into oncoming traffic. Horns blared as cars slammed on their brakes, causing a major pile up.

Rock rode Tara all the way to Griffin, pulling up on Tony, who had moved to a house in Backline. His crib had always been a safe haven for the troublemakers in the family, a trend Flame started when he was ten.

They parked Bang-Bang's truck in the backyard and covered it with a tarp. Inside, they chilled on the living room couch, scrolling through their contacts for a ride to The Spot. A few dead ends later, Rock hit Jayvo, who was at a dog fight on Roundtree Road. He was up next, but assured him he would slide through when things wrapped up.

As they waited for Jayvo, they fired up a blunt, listening to Tony talk shit about how he only saw his cousins when they had done some fuck shit. They gave Tony his own blunt to shut him up, but that didn't help.

He lit it on the stove and returned to the living room. "So what the fuck you done did now, wit'cha hot ass? You done did something. That's why you hidin' that damn car."

Rock sucked his teeth. "Man, go 'head with that bullshit, ain't nobody done nothing."

"Mmm hmm." He eyed Rock suspiciously as he hit the blunt, exhaling through his nose. He turned to Bang-Bang. "Well, let me borrow your truck, then. I need to go get me a pack of cigarettes. I'm nickin' like a mu'fucka!"

He cut his eyes at Rock, who shook his head inconspicuously. "My shit really fucked up, right now. Willie is supposed to come look at it tomorrow."

"And a lie don't care who tells it. Ain't shit wrong with your mu'fuckin' car and you know it! Y'all done did something and y'all hidin'!" Tony said. "So for hiding at my house it's gon' cost ya. You know the routine." He stuck his hand out.

Rock sucked his teeth. "You never used to charge Flame." He reached in his sock, peeled off two twenty dollar bills from a folded stack, and held it out.

"I ain't have to. He kept me straight." He snatched the money and turned to Bang-Bang, who was busy texting someone, and held out his hand. "You ain't excluded!"

Smiling and shaking his head, Bang-Bang pulled his bankroll from his pocket and peeled him off.

Forty minutes later, Jayvo pulled up and they left out of the house. On the way to the car, Rock told Bang-Bang that he texted Huncho, and was waiting for him to return his call.

They hopped in Jayvo's car and headed to The Spot.

CHAPTER 9

Huncho and Camry were at Club Encore, a club in Wynn Hotel's. They were at one of the 95 V.I.P. tables, enjoying the entertainment. Huncho was sipping XO, while Camry drank juice. They had been at the casino earlier, where he let Camry blow a few stacks at the crap and roulette tables.

For the last few days they had checked out several different hotels, casinos, and clubs. At the Luxor hotel they dined at a restaurant called The Cat House. They had an intimate setting and live entertainment, Camry's treat to him for being good. He almost choked when he saw the near naked women that served as the entertainment.

The next day they went to the Simon Restaurant and Lounge inside Palms Palace, where they stayed in a sixteen hundred dollar a night condo. It was attached to a hotel. Later on, they took a stroll down Freemont Street, known as the Old School Vegas because it was where Vegas had started.

Club Encore had been the best yet. It was a place to chill, enjoy, and relax. Besides the 95 V.I.P. tables, there were thirty cabanas on two levels and day beds that surrounded a beautiful pool, where you could get a massage while relaxing. Becoming accustomed to being pampered with massages, Camry was all smiles.

The trip took her mind off the kidnapping, but when Huncho proposed, it blew her mind. He slid a 4 1/2 karat platinum engagement ring on her finger, one with princess cut baguette diamonds. It was the most beautiful thing she had ever seen, and the tears that fell from her eyes showed it. Huncho caught her staring at the ring and smiled.

He knew she loved it.

But as he sat at the table sipping XO, his mind was on business back home. He had left Rock in charge of his operation.

Camry placed her hand on his forearm. "What's on your mind, baby?"

"Nothing really, I was just thinking about my nigga D-Day." He ran his hand down his face. "His mama left a message on my phone. His appeal got denied."

"I'm sorry to hear that. Does that mean he can't get out?"

He took a sip of XO. "I don't know, baby. I ain't e'en talked to his people yet. I just got the message. I'ma find a lawyer that can help him when we get back."

Back in their condo bedroom, Huncho sat on the edge of the bed, checking his messages while Camry showered. He had one from his mother about needing seven hundred for rent, and another from Rock, telling him to hit his line ASAP. Something was up. Having promised Camry not to let his phone interrupt their vacation, he had left special instructions not to call him unless it was an emergency.

Taking advantage of Camry's shower preoccupation, he got up from the bed and stepped out on the balcony to return Rock's call.

He answered on the second ring. "Nard is no longer with the living."

A loud silence followed.

Fed conscious, Huncho played it cool. "Sorry to hear that. I'll be home in a day or two."

He hung up, in somewhat of a daze, eyes blurred by the Las Vegas skyline. Staring out over Sin City, a metropolitan structure built and ran by the Mob, it dawned on him how each human wrote the scroll of their own life, each page bearing two sides: what they would like to be and what they actually would be.

So while we may know who we are now, who we could become the next moment was unknown to us. His fate was undeniable proof of this fact.

Less than a year ago, he had been a convicted felon with a life sentence. Now he stood tall, feeling like a young don in a black and gold Versace shirt, matching slacks, tailored to fit perfectly over his Mauri's.

All because he hadn't let his dreams come true.

He made them!

Big facts.

Nevertheless, the power money possessed and yielded to its possessor no longer excited him. How could it when it clearly came with a price? That ever-present drop of poison in every shining moment of happiness.

That knowledge that pain will come again.

Always...

Money kept the Southside divided, got his baby mama kidnapped, his partnas and enemies killed, and had caused him much more stress than he felt it was worth.

Yet and still...

"Thinking about me?" Camry cooed behind him.

He turned around to find her standing in a sexy pose with her hand on her hip, wearing black LA Perla lingerie and a pair Sergio Ross stilettoes. He smiled and walked into the condo, unbuttoning his shirt.

***

The Gate, a club on Tara formally known as J-Paul's, was the Mafia's establishment of choice for the night. Thoroughly searched, they crossed the threshold rocking diamond chains with "MAFIA MADE" pendants, an inner circle trend TD popped off.

In the back, they shook their dreads to the club music, throwing up the M's as 2-DUB bounced around, waving grey bandannas in the air.

They were lit. Blunt smoking. Bottle popping. Bad bitches of every ethnicity, piped, taking full advantage of the free bud and liquor available to all. Not to mention the presence of certain Mafiosos who had been M.I.A. due to the heavy drug trafficking.

Having shot security an extra twenty bucks at the door, even Thugga was on the scene. He was spittin' game at a group of female co-eds, attendees of Clayton State University. Booman, Woadie's latest initiate, was drunk out of his mind. The same age as Thugga, he had been subjected to the twenty dollar fee as well and got a real kick out of buying liquor. It had become somewhat of a weekend ritual for him since the club's grand opening.

Trigga Mafia fell off in the club in celebration of Mickey's birthday. Swamp deep, they outnumbered 2-DUB Mafia two to one, easy. Rocking blue jeans, "FREE TMC MEL" shirts, and gold bandannas, they took to the stage to perform "Pistol Grip", a recent track they'd released, dissing Murk Mob and M.O.B. 23.

Peeping 2DM in the club, they channeled the disrespect their way. Their energy had the club live. Some of them rocked hockey masks with gold dreads. They walked offstage, muggin'.

The tension rose as the night progressed until Skeet, a boney, tar-skinned TMC affiliate with nappy hair, threw a Corona bottle, hitting Tall-Teezzee hard on the shoulder from behind.

"Da fuck!" Tall-Teezzee wiped beer from his face and shirt. "Oh, hell naw!"

Thugga and Booman were on it, moving with purpose, pushing and shoving their way through the crowd. Jayvo, TD, Bang-Bang, and Fat Mike flanked them, tucking their chains into their shirts. A club patron was taking his drink to the head when Bang-Bang snatched it in passing, taking a sip as they proceeded.

Champ stepped frontline, sliding Skeet behind him. To his right was his brother, Ron-Meezy. Standing tall, arms folded across his chest, he was ready for whatever. His orange streaked dreads hung neck length, covering the "R.I.P. ACE" tattoo. He had lost his "Day One" to this war and still felt some type of way. He grilled Thugga through narrowed slits.

"What's up?" Thugga said.

Gino nudged Ron from behind and slipped him a hunting knife. "Whatever you want to be up, fuck boy!"

Jayvo stepped in front of Thugga. "Hold up, brah, you tri-"

Champ cut Jayvo short with an uppercut-right hook-straight jab combo, sending him backward into the Mafiosos. Bang-Bang smashed the bottle across Champ's head, dropping him to the floor.

The club went kaboom.

Fists swinging. Feet stomping. Chairs flying. Pool cues whacking. Bottles bashing.

2DM found themselves on the worse end of the ass whoopin', but didn't back down.

Thugga and Skeet went blow-for-blow. Skeet's nose was leaking. Thugga's eye was a li'l swollen and his lip was busted. Catching sight of the action from long range, Dee-Dee shot across the floor, blindsiding Thugga with a mean right, sending him barreling left. Bouncing off the wall, he charged at Dee-Dee, only to be thrown in a yoke by Gino. He gasped for breath, pulling at Gino's arm, trying with all his might to free himself.

Ron-Meezy ran up and stabbed Thugga in the neck, leaving the knife in. Dark crimson blood poured down his entire left side. "That's for my nigga Ace."

The club lights came on, the music stopped, and security rushed through the crowd, yoking affiliates from both 2-DUB and Trigga Mafia into chokeholds. Trigga Mafia was too deep, so unable to control them physically, they began using their pepper spray to disperse the crowd. Everyone stampeded to the door to escape the cough-provoking chemicals, clearing the floor. Left bleeding from the mouth, security found Thugga. After taking a closer look, they realized his neck, arms, and chest were also bleeding from stab wounds. An ambulance was called immediately, but not before Thugga took his last breath. He died on the dirty floor of J-Paul's.

***

"He was very lucky," Dr. Modzelewski, a blonde hair white female doctor told Ms. Evans, standing outside her son's hospital room. "The bullet that entered his side could've been fatal if it had hit his heart. We were able to remove the bullet, but the damage done to his lungs will require that he use a breathing machine for the time being."

Ms. Evans's tired eyes watered as she took in the news. She had been at the hospital for nearly two days while her son Nard underwent surgery after surgery. He had been on the passenger side while Della drove the day Rock and Bang-Bang had caught him in traffic. Della, who had been hit in the head, died before the Range Rover crashed into another car and swerved off road. As a result, Nard's back was nearly broken, and his eye was lost to flying glass.

“Well, do you think he’ll walk again?” Ms. Evans sniveled, wiping a cascading tear from her cheek.

Dr. Modzelewski hesitated before sighing. “Honestly, right now, it’s too early to tell.” She placed a hand on her shoulder. “My best advice to you is go home and get some rest. You know, put it in God’s hands.”

News hit the street of Nard’s survival, and Huncho was livid. Rock thought Nard was driving the Range Rover. His eyes were on Bang-Bang when Della and Nard walked out of Zaxby’s. Rock was furious as well because he had killed an innocent female and allowed his intended target to live. Now the ongoing beef between the two cliques were the talk of the streets, with Thugga being its latest casualty, Trigga Mafia’s retaliation for the hit on Nard. The war had drawn police attention to the streets and due to the pressure being applied to bring in Della’s killer, known members of each crew had begun to be picked up for questioning. On every news channel, Della’s picture was being shown as they talked about her accomplishments as an aspiring college student and promising career cut short by a senseless gang-related shooting.

“This shit ain’t good, brah,” Huncho said after the news station went to another story. He shook his head and changed the channel.

“What Bang-Bang do with his car?”

“He took it to Florida to get it painted,” Rock said. “He didn’t want to get it done up here so he left about three this morning.”

Huncho pinched the bridged of his nose, releasing a heavy sigh. “We gon’ have to get a new spot with all this shit going on. Ain’t no telling when them folks might hit this mu’fucka. Any word on Nard?”

Rock blew out a stream of smoke, double-coughing from the potent Cali bud. "Last I heard he was still in Southern Regional."

Huncho began dropping money in the book bag Rock had brought to the spot, full of the money made while he'd been in Vegas. He found himself sad for some unexplainable reason and could not rack his brain as to why, until it hit him. It was deja vu. Only three years ago, Flame had been his right hand, whereas now it was Flame's younger cousin, the last time the Mafia had to relocate The Spot.

Huncho knew he had to keep his face out of the streets or his name would pop up sooner or later. Subsequently, he decided to take Dreak and his girlfriend, Arielle, along on a vacation with his family.

Dreak had just recently finished recording his first project with Break Free Records, a mixtape to be called "What They Didn't Tell You". As a treat, Huncho had him ask Arielle what her dream vacation was, to which she replied a relaxation trip to the Virgin Islands. Less than a week later, the vacation was nothing short of a dream come true. All the while, Huncho made it his business to see to it that Dreak got all the credit, making it seem as though the success of his mixtape had paid the expenses. With her lack of intel on Huncho's side dealings outside the music industry, not to mention all the show's Dreak had been showing up to perform at, it wasn't too hard to finesse. She was all smiles, leaving the airport, as she bragged to her friends about how she wouldn't be able to join them this weekend at the Riverdale Cinema due to her man taking her on an all expense paid trip to the Caribbean for no other reason than to fulfill her fantasy. Unbeknownst to her, Dreak hadn't been paid for a show, since signing with Break Free.

To get his face out there, TD and Huncho had been signing him up for every amateur and open mic night at every bar, club, party, and event, on every side of town in the Metro Atlanta area. They had even gone as far as to book him for an Major Distribution Label sponsored talent show, held in the center of Southlake Mall. He didn't win, but his performance their had gained him a lot of exposure. The presence of label executives, company A&R's, and prominent recording artist like T.I, Young Jeezy, and Ludacris, to name a few, had brought media attention to the event that countless aspiring dream chasers of every kind prayed for, but only one-in-a-million received. Needless to say, he was gaining local celebrity status fast.

Nard's shooting didn't worry Huncho; he had an alibi. His only worry was the police getting in his business and learning of the money he was making in the street. The situation was quickly escalating into something that could lead to a federal investigation. He had nothing to cover up his illegal activities. This was so serious that he had put a direct hold on avenging Thugga's death, a decision that Rock wasn't too happy about but he understood.

To keep the Mafia an ongoing concern, Huncho had restructured the movement upon a concept known as Familism. He'd discovered it in an old La Costra Nostra book he read during one of his frequent trips to the hole in prison. The principle of the concept is based on a system that doesn't place the needs or wants of one person as an individual, before the needs, wants, or well-being of an organization as a whole, the syndicate in this case being 2DM. It was out of his hands. As bad as Rock wanted blood, Huncho had no choice but to deny his request for an immediate retaliation, explaining to him the importance of a leader practicing what they preach.

"I gotta be fair when it comes to governing our affairs," he told Rock. "In order for an example to be followed, one must be set. That's just real."

Leaving Rock, he picked up Tall-Teezzee and Woadie and made a couple more stops to pick up some food and funds, before heading home to put the money up. Zakayla and Camry were at her mother's house, so he called Dreak and told him he was on his way. Together they drove to 5-4-3 Studios, an establishment owned by Purp, all the more motivation to bring Dreak along.

Having his artist with him provided the perfect explanation for his visit, if ever the Feds inquired. One thing Huncho had learned, and taught himself to do on instinct, was to think and plan ahead, being sure to take all possibilities, both negative and positive, into consideration. His logic: Better to be sensible, than senseless.

They arrived to find Purp in the middle of a session with 3rd Degree, a group of young niggas from Hunter's Ridge, a Jonesboro neighborhood off Tara Road. They were another one of Purp's music industry investments.

He was behind the mixing board, bobbing his head to one of the bass-driven tracks the group, who now sat lounging on the comfy studio sectional behind him, had just recorded. All three of them were dark-skinned, with shoulder-length dreads.

Purp turned around as Huncho and Dreak entered and waved them over with a smile.

Recognizing one of the members of 3rd Degree from around the way, Dreak approach him, and showed love, embracing him with a quick handshake-hug.

He pulled back. "A-R Dreaded, right? House party in Bonanza. You spoke up for me. Hit ya bro, and got me a One."

A-R Dreaded was the younger brother of B-Star Gotti, a major M.O.B 23 Hard affiliate. They're headquarters was a hood in Lovejoy called, Bonanza. Having an allegiance with Murk Mob, a clique from Pointe South Parkway, they too had beef with 2-DUB Mafia. It was smash on sight. That night at a house party off Cardinal, his image having been associated with 2DM, mistake or not, Dreak found himself caught up in the senseless madness he had tried so hard to avoid.

A-R smiled, shaking his head back to toss his dreads from his line of vision. "Shiiid, I had to. You got jumped, took yo ass whoopin', got up, went outside in the front yard and still called niggas out for Ones. I knew my brother would respect that shit. On some real Southside shit, a nigga gotta respect it. A solid nigga, anyways. What that whole thing was 'bout anyways?"

"They thought I was 2DM, but I'm not. The label I'm signed to just so happens to be founded by some well known Mafiosos." Dreak waved it off. "Ever since I was seen on stage with the 2-DUB and Southside Mafia at that Southlake Mall talent gig, I been catchin' smoke the worst way.

"Naw," A-R said. "You bullshitin'."

"Shiiid, like hell! My name got mentioned in a 2-DUB Mafia diss song. Somebody spray painted 'Fuck Dreak Gottem' on the side of Buster's. And just the other day I got shot at by some Murk Mob niggas, leaving a block party in Bradford Park. Only reason I'm good on Da Grove is cause my girl got a cousin in Hit Squad, so they know what's up wit' me."

"Goddamn, bra-bra!" A-R laughed. "You better get'cha self a tool. Gotta keep the tool! I thought I had beef, but you got me beat. You cant go nowhere!"

Dreak sucked his teeth. "Naw man, niggas got me fucked up! Aint no place I can't go. I'm built for whatever's comin' for me. Is it bout all that? Hell naw! Not the slightest bit. But I will take it there. And won't be fucked up bout it. Really and truly, I just want the money. The paper, man. That's what it's all bout, but these niggas so simple-minded, its like they done forgot. The clique era came to be in an attempt to get signed. To get that paper! This extra shit they on now, this shootin' and killin', maaan, niggas throwin' they life away 'bout nothin', and the sad truth is that they aint e'en conscious of it. Yea, sometimes I wanna click and go ham, but I gotta think for these niggas." Dreak sighed. "All the shit I been through lately, though, I might as well be throwin' the M's up."

A-R shrugged. "Why don't you? Huncho fuck wit'cha! Heard him tell Purp, myself, that you like the lil brother he never had. Big bra got mad love for you. Real talk."

"I don't know." Dreak paused, turning to look over his shoulder at Huncho and Purp, both of whom were bobbing their heads to the track Purp was mixing in the absence of his engineer. He turned back to A-R Dreaded, brows furrowed in deep thought. He knew Huncho liked him, but to hear the love he had for him expressed to that extent, outside his presence, to individuals he hadn't known he fucked with, thereby erasing the possibility of an ulterior motive for the sharing of such heartfelt statements in reference to him, he looked at Huncho in a new light. His grandma always said that sometimes caring can touch where words couldn't reach. He now understood why. Any nigga can say what they want, but the real in his blood. Same for a female. He had only just begun to live his life, technically, but even before the streets he had learned an objective fact about human behavior: People tell you what they want you to hear. With that understanding he knew what Huncho had said in that moment was genuine. There bond had grown deeper than the money.

Expression still distant, Dreak shrugged, shaking his head. "My grandfather once told me something I'll never forget. Something I keep in mind with all that I do. He said the results of our lives today are the sum total of thoughts, actions, and decisions we made in our past. Therefore the results of our future will be the sum total of thoughts, actions and decisions that we make today in the present. He told me no matter what, always make the best decision. He stressed that. And you know what?"

"W'sup?" A-R had been hanging on his every word.

Dreak looked A-R in his eyes. "Now, that's how I make a living."

"These young niggas gone be the next Hotboyz, yo!" Purp sat with a fat Philly burning in hand. "That li'l nigga right there ain't nothing but twelve. They call 'em Spazz." Purp pointed to one of the group members, seated on the sectional behind them, and turned a knob, raising the volume. Huncho was truly impressed. The baby-faced young'un was smirking hard, unable to contain himself as he watched them nod to his lyrics. His bars had even got Dreak's attention, ending his conversation with A-R, he made his way over to the mixing board, standing beside Huncho.

"Damn, Purp, you got you some fire spittas up in here, don't you?" Huncho said.

"I do. He just finished stacking his verse and doin' his adlibs. Don't even take long to mix, his sound's so butter!" Purp spent his armchair around.

"So, the infamous Dreak, we meet again. How's it feel to be somewhat of a local celeb? Know your practically beatin' the ladies off with a stick by now."

"You know what Da Dale goin' on!" Dreak said.

"What Da Dale g- Maaan," Purp bust out laughing.

"Naw, though, seriously. They most definitely at a young nigga, but what's new?" Dreak said. "I got my baby. She all I need. We came from nothin' together. I got her for life. I'll never switch up on her. Not for money, and damn sure not for another piece of pussy."

Purp nodded, caught off guard by such devotion to a female at a young age. Yet, he wasn't convinced. "We'll see how you feel once you start touring."

Dreak shrugged, deciding to himself not to dispute. He knew how it was, but he was different. He didn't expect most people to understand. "Hey, what can I say? She's who I do it for. Her and my grandma. They're all I got."

Again, Purp nodded, but this time, he remained silent. He initially thought that Dreak was whipped, but he didn't get that vibe from him now. It was something else. He couldn't put his finger on it, but something about Dreak seemed…certain. Like he knew what he wanted in life. Or like his whole life had already been planned, mapped out by he himself, and no one, regardless of fame and fortune, could influence him to deviate from his pre-planned-self-imposed life objectives. He was clearly determined, a rare trait found amongst his age. Then again, so was his talent.

A first impression had been made.

Huncho was in good spirits. "Yeah, I was just bringin' Dreak through to check out ya spot since this is where he'll be recording his next project.

"That's what's up," Purp said with a curt nod. "Matter fact, while you're here, let's put 'em on this song with my boys and see what he got." He looked at Dreak. "'Sup, you ready?"

"Maaaan, I stay ready! Just let me hear the track."

Purp hit a few buttons on the board and the song started over. Leaving Dreak and 3rd Degree to do their thing, he and Huncho went into an office to discuss his next purchase. There was no need to mention his current beef. He informed Purp instead about his trips to Vegas and Cali, concluding the conversation by setting a time and date for the fifteen bricks to be delivered.

***

Thugga was laid to rest a few days later and the Mafia stuck out like sore thumbs. They weren't the only ones that stuck out, though. In the crowd were undercovers. County or federal, Huncho was unsure, but either way, it wasn't good. The following day he placed a lawyer on retainer.

***

Razor heard about Nard being shot and involved in a wreck and abandoned Plan A, which was for him to lead Nard to Huncho so he could kill him, or at the least, have him killed. He was going to show Nard where Huncho laid his head at, the place called The Spot. With Nard out of commission, he had no other choice but to resort to Plan B, which involved him making an anonymous call to the police, implicating Huncho and his most trusted Mafioso's in the car wash shooting, Ace's murder, the triple murders of Hollywood, Fresh, and Pee-Wee, and Nard's shooting, even going as far as telling the authorities about his drug dealings. He knew for a fact they would be picked up once he revealed details about the murders that only a person involved would know. He was counting on it. Damn, the G-Code, Omerta, and any other code of silence recognized by certified street niggas. This was the only win he saw for himself. His mind was set.

He had to do, what he had to do.

Between the gunshot wounds and the injuries from the wreck, Nard had to undergo a total of six surgeries. He was back to talking a little, yet he was still heavily sedated, so his conservations were short and barely audible. His mother stayed by his bedside as much as possible. A few of his boys came to see him as well. He still didn't know Della was dead, or that he had missed her funeral. All that he remembered was being in a car crash. In his mind, his injuries stemmed from the wreck alone. He was unaware that the accident was no accident or that it had been caused by someone shooting into his truck.

"You want something to drink, baby?" Ms. Evans poured ice water from the plastic container into a cup, stuck a straw in it, and put it into his mouth before Nard could say yes or no. He took a few small sips. "How you feeling?" she asked. Nard nodded his head.

Ms. Evans began to rattle off all the things Dr. Modzelewski had told her, leaving out the part about him never walking again. His pelvis had been so severely damaged that it was unrepairable, leaving him a cripple for life. The damage to his back had rendered him paralyzed from the waist down.

"Where's Della?" Nard mumbled. "Is she okay?"

The look in his mother's eyes immediately told him she wasn't. She shook her head. "The doctor said she was dead before the car even crashed."

"Dead before the crash?" Nard was confused. "How?"

"She was shot in the head, baby," she said, rubbing his arm lightly as if it would ease the pain. "You were also shot twice. The police said someone pulled up next to y'all and began shooting into the truck. They think you were the intended target."

A mixed expression of fear and anger appeared on his face as the realization of what happened hit home. 2-DUB Mafia had been trying to take him out, but had instead killed Della. He knew the Mafia was behind the attempt on his life, and tried to remember if they had been followed. He never heard the gunshots because the music was up too loud. All he remembered was crashing and trying to duck, and right before the crash, the driver side window fell in. Della fell towards him and a burgundy-looking car was beside them. He remembered, and then it all went blank. Now he knew why Della had been slumped over his lap.

"It's been some detective coming by to talk to you and they left a card with a number on it. Told me to call once you were able to talk. Do you want to talk to them now, or wait until you get a li'l better?" his mother asked.

He shook his head, in response.

Later that afternoon, a few of his homeboys came through and let him know what was going on in the streets.

After they left, he laid on the hospital cot, reflecting on all that he had been told that day. When the nurse came in to change his bandages and check his vitals, he asked why he couldn't feel anything in his legs or feet. She told him that he had been paralyzed from the injuries to his back and spine.

CHAPTER 11

"El estado del hasta reunirse mi luego desde ahí acompañar nosotras alla's," Ricardo stated. "Suyo niña amiga querer ser con él."

"Musitar ellas querer ser acogida," Carlo replied.

Ricardo told Carlo that Huncho was going to meet him, then go with him, and that his girlfriend would be present. Carlo said that they were welcome. When they ended the call, Ricardo headed in the direction of the restaurant he was to be meeting Huncho.

On the West Coast for business, once again, Huncho had brought Camry along to do some shopping on the famous Rodeo Drive. He was meeting up with Ricardo to deliver the money for the weed copping and the handlers that made sure his packages were properly wrapped and sealed. He didn't mind spending the extra couple of thousand dollars to make sure his package made it to its destination.

They had been in Cali for two days and it was their final day before returning home. After meeting up with Ricardo and handling business, they drove out to Rodeo Drive and began a $15,000 shopping spree. They went to the Chanel, Gucci, Fendi, and Louis Vuitton stores, as well as a few others and a couple boutiques. They were amazed at how different the stores were back home. They stopped for lunch at an expensive steak house and had a bottle of Pinot Noir, which is the Victoria's Secret of wines, along with their steak and pasta.

Every place they went, they snapped pictures for memories of them being on the famous shopping strip. They bumped into a few stars that were out shopping and hiding behind dark sunglasses. When they were done, they went back to the room to pack, then drove the rented 550 Benz to the airport.

When they arrived back in Atlanta hours later, they picked Zakayla up from Huncho's mother's house. He dropped them off and went to check on Purp. When he pulled away from his house, he noticed a dark-colored SUV pulling out behind him, trailing from a distance. He didn't know if it was 12 or not, but he wasn't taking any chances, so he cocked the 40-cal and drove with it in his hand, remembering how Nard had been caught slipping. He called back home and told Camry to make sure that the alarm was set in a way that didn't make it seem like anything was wrong.

He drove at a consistent speed, keeping the SUV in his sight, to make them think he didn't know that he was being followed. He drove at a consistent speed, keeping the SUV in his sight to make them think he didn't know that he was being followed. He had felt like he was being watched while he was in Cali, but had shook it off. As he thought about his flight back home, he had had the same feeling. Once when he got up to use the restroom, he had locked eyes with a guy that he could have sworn that he had known from somewhere. Now as he drove, he was trying to put a name to the face.

His phone began to ring as he pulled up to a red light and he checked the screen. Seeing that it was a private number, he allowed it to go to voicemail. He checked the rearview mirror and saw that the SUV was behind him, with only one car between them. His phone rang again as the light turned green. He made a quick left on Taylor Road. The SUV made the same turn. He sent the blocked call to voicemail. He was slowing to a stop at the four-way traffic light by Riverdale High School, thinking of how only yesterday the truancy officer had told him and Flame that the route they were headed they'd both wind up dead or in jail. Huncho shook his head, his heart growing heavy as he thought about how he had failed his Day-

1 by allowing Thugga, Flame's younger cousin, to fall victim to the streets.

"I'ma beat the odds for us, my nigga," he said, aloud to his fallen friend. "And I promise, if it's the last thing I do, I'ma set ya family straight. Thug, he just- he wouldn't listen, bro." Huncho punched the steering wheel. "Damn it, Thug! What the fuck!"

He shot another glance in the rearview mirror at the suspicious SUV.

Just as he was about to lay his phone in his lap, a tan Explorer with dark tints cut in front of him, blocking his path, causing him to slam on his brakes at the light. "What the fuck!" he yelled, instantly knowing he was in trouble at the sight of the barrel of an AK-47 sticking out of the window. "Oh shit!" Quickly, he snatched the gear in reverse, raised the 40-cal, and started shooting through his windshield at the Explorer.

The gunman toting the stick had let off a few rounds, leaving steam coming from the hood of Huncho's Escalade, but was forced to duck back inside under heavy fire from .40 Cal shots. The traffic behind him swerved out of the way to avoid a collision. Huncho slammed on the brakes again, snatched the gear back in drive, and smashed out down Roberts Drive. His engine was giving out as he sped down the street and his sight was limited due to the damage he had done to his windshield when shooting at the Explorer and the nigga with the AK.

Two sets of headlights appeared behind him, gaining fast. He grabbed his phone, which had fallen on the floor as he drove. He got a spare clip for his 40 from the console. He turned a corner and slammed on the brakes, then bailed out of the truck.

Once out of the truck, he hit the woods in a sprint, bypassing a cut known to all as "The Kitchen," and came out in the next subdivision. He knew his truck would be traced back to him and Camry, so all he could do to cover himself from being locked up was to dial 911 and play his part.

***

Federal agents stormed Club 5-4-3 and the studio simultaneously with a federal search warrant. The day shift at the club along with the few customers were all searched and restrained.

The entire search lasted a couple of hours and all that was found were a few guns and a couple of bags of weed that were being smoked out of. Purp's computers were also confiscated from the offices of both the club and studio. When the raids began, he had been in the studio working with 3rd Degree. A Glock 45 and an ounce of Kush had been found laying next to the mixing board, and the field agent working the scene, a young white guy with sandy blonde hair and cold grey eyes, Agent Smith, quickly pinned it on him. With a look and nod, his engineer quickly claimed both the weed and gun, knowing that he would be well compensated for taking the charges.

"Like I said, I don't own a gun or know anything about drugs, Agent!" Purp stated sarcastically from the floor, where he laid bound with flexi-cuffs.

Agent Smith stood looking at him as if he wanted to kick him in the face. "Get him outta here!" he ordered, pointing at the audio engineer that had taken the charges for Purp.

"Call me soon as you get a bond. My lawyer will be up there before you even get booked in," Purp said to the engineer as he was led out of the room.

Out of sight, Purp looked back up at Agent Smith.

"Now if you're not charging me with anything, you need to remove these restraints so I can call my attorneys and let them know how you have come in my place of business harassing me, my people, and have three minors on the floor with guns pointed in their faces."

Agent Smith's face turned beet red at the blatant display of sarcasm. He thought he had Purp on a firearm charge that would get his probation revoked and a five year sentence for being a convicted felon with a gun. He would've been happy to get him off the street for just a short time, but Purp had outsmarted him again.

"Get them off the floor and un-cuff them!" Agent Smith ordered, then stood face to face with Purp as his restraints were being removed. "I'm going to get your ass, and when I do, I promise you'll be so old by the time you get out that your dick won't even get hard!" he threatened through clenched teeth.

Purp smiled in Smith's face. "I don't think your wife would like that, and I know your daughter wouldn't, the way she sucked this big black muthafucker last night... Now get the fuck out of my building and off my property!" Purp yelled, losing the smile, holding Smith's gaze. "And that's an order!"

***

At the same time, on the other side of the map, Carlos's ranch was being raided along with Ricardo's house. Carlos wasn't as lucky because 75 bricks and a half a million dollars were found on the property. Ricardo's luck ran out too when they both realized the Mexicans they had been dealing with were undercover D.E.A. agents. They had enough evidence on the two brothers to put them away for life. Besides the sales that were made and drugs that were found, they were also hit with the RICO Act and C.C.E., running a continued criminal enterprise, and Huncho was in several of the surveillance pictures.

***

Mel had taken a bullet in the arm the night that he had tried to take Huncho out. The bullet wound was what gave him away as being one of the people involved in the murder attempt. When he went to the hospital, the police were instantly notified since he was a gunshot victim. He was held for questioning, and when his story didn't sound right, the officers quickly did a check to see if any shooting had been reported within the last hour of his appearing at the hospital. They instantly linked him to the shoot-out that Huncho was involved in. When Huncho was brought in to identify him, he assured the police that they had the wrong man, so Mel had been released.

Since the shooting, he had been staying at his mother's house until he healed up, not mentioning that he was broke and had nowhere else to go. His girl had left him once he got out and could no longer take care of her. He ended up jumping on her, which turned out to be his worst mistake.

After leaving Mel, she bumped into Bang-Bang at a gas station and exchanged numbers. She found out he was 2-DUB Mafia, and she told him everything she knew about Mel, even where his mother stayed. Bang-Bang hadn't acted on the information that she had provided for two reasons. The first was when he told Huncho about what he had found out, Huncho did not make a move on him because as soon as he marked the nigga, the bitch would start feeling sorry and tell it. Then the second reason was because of the heat that was on them and the situation. But now that Mel had made an attempt on Huncho's life, he had issued Mel's death warrant and sent his two gunman to serve it.

The sun had just set. Woadie slid in the front seat of the Toyota Camry and began peeling the steering column. Forty-five seconds later, he was starting the engine and pulling off.

Bang-Bang stepped out into the street and hopped in. They were both high from snorting coke and little was said between the two of them. Woadie stopped by his crib and got his AK-47 and AR-15, which he gave to Bang-Bang, and they headed towards Mel's mother's house after snorting some more coke.

Mel had just returned from Grady Memorial after visiting Nard. They had talked briefly about the failed attempt on Huncho's life, while Nard's mother was out of the room. Nard had assured him that the money was still available if he succeeded in killing Huncho. Nard expressed how badly he wanted it done with tears in his eyes as he explained how he would never walk again. He knew Huncho was responsible for his predicament. As he expressed himself, Mel had been unable to look at him face to face.

As he sat on his mother's back porch, he thought about how Nard was laid up in the hospital, unable to move. He felt Nard's pain, but his misfortune wasn't what mortified Mel. It was Nard's money that had him at Huncho's throat. In all actuality, he didn't give a fuck about Nard. He knew that he was a snake and had heard the rumors about him snitching. The only reason he fucked with Nard in the first place was because at the time he was broke and Nard was putting niggas on.

He put the last twist on the Swisher then rolled the end of it in the flame that shot up from the Bic lighter. As he slowly rolled the end of the blunt back and forth in the flame, he thought about his brother. It was another reason he held a grudge against Nard. He had always felt that he and Pit had been sent on a Section 8 dummy mission that ended up costing Pit his life at the end. As a result of his brother's death, he also ended up losing his life too, in a sense, because now he was facing a murder charge that he had no intentions of ever going back to court to face. His ticket to freedom had eluded him.

He needed the money that Nard was willing to pay for murdering Huncho, like a sinner on his last breath needed more time. He would use the money to leave the state and reestablish himself elsewhere. He thought of other alternatives to get some money up, and the main one was robbing and laying some niggas down. He had also considered just going all out and saying fuck it and running up in a bank. If he made it, he would leave town immediately, and if not, he would die in the muthafucka holding court on the spot.

He raised the blunt to his lips to hit it and just as he did, a loud clash inside the house caught his attention. Hopping up, he peeked through the back door window, but saw nothing. After hitting the blunt once more, he stubbed it out and went in to check on his mother, figuring that she had dropped something. He crossed the kitchen and headed to the living room, and just as he turned the corner, he was hit square in the face with the stock of the assault rifle Woadie held.

He tumbled backwards, reaching up at his broken nose and split forehead as he fell. Woadie aimed the chopper down at him and ordered him to crawl in the living room, where Bang-Bang had his mother lying face down on the floor with the AR-15 pointed at the back of her head as she sobbed silently. When he saw that his mother was being held at gunpoint, he began to beg and plead that she be released unharmed. He knew that he was about to die with a surety when he looked and saw that it was Bang-Bang who held his mother. He knew that Bang-Bang was a killer and had earned the name Bang-Bang from busting his guns.

"Brah, let my moms go, shawdy. She ain't got nothing to do with this," he started to say, but the words were cut short by four thunderous claps of the AR-15 and he witnessed his mother's head exploding. He went into a rage and attempted to get off the floor, but was knocked a few feet back when Woadie and Bang-Bang both squeezed the triggers of their guns simultaneously.

The bullets ripped chunks off his face and chin as they walked up on his body, letting off round after round. The cocaine that they were on sent them into a murderous daze. Mel's dead body jerked and flopped with each bullet that tore into his flesh. Before they fled the scene, Mel had been hit over twenty-five times from head to feet. It was their way of saying and letting the next mu'fucka's know "don't fuck with the Mafia!"

CHAPTER 12

Dumbway and the other Mafiosos behind the wall had been hearing about the murders and the attempt on Huncho's life. They weren't happy to hear it, but were glad to know the Mafia was back riding for the cause. Each of them had talked to Huncho, but due to the monitored calls, the conversations were always strained and limited. They were never able to get straight to the point and tell what they wanted to say, so they did the best they could, talking in codes and slang.

Huncho had been sending Southside Queens to the prison to see them, and each trip they made, they were strapped with balloons of weed. Dumbway had bribed a female officer to sneak a cell phone to him and promised to pay her for her help. She had finally agreed, and he told her he would get back with her after he hollered at his people on the outside. The same day he had sent Huncho a letter describing the situation.

Two weeks had passed after sending the second letter out to Huncho with the info he needed to make it happen. He had talked to Huncho after sending the first and he assured him that he would make it happen. But it had been two weeks and hadn't nothing shook for him. He began to think the officer had reneged and kept the money and the phone. She hadn't worked his dormitory in over a week and when he did happen to see her elsewhere, it was as if he didn't even exist. He didn't want to confront her because if she was playing the game raw and cutthroat, she could have him fucked up.

"Inmate Washington, report to the laundry," a white male officer yelled into the dormitory as he wrote out a pass, standing in the doorway.

He untied the do-rag on his head, stuck it in his locker, and then checked himself in the mirror before going up to the officer to get his pass. After leaving out of the dormitory he took the long way to the laundry, stopping to holler at some of his homeboys here and there who were out road dogging, standing in the window of their dormitory or out on the wellness walk. By the time he made it to the laundry building, a couple inmates stood out front on their smoke break. He walked up to the counter and laid his pass on top of it and another inmate took it to the back.

"Let me see your I.D. card," ordered a female voice with a little attitude, causing him to turn back to the counter. "You are inmate Washington, aren't you?" she added.

"Yeah, this me!" he replied as he put his prison I.D. on the counter.

She turned and walked off with his card and pass in hand. Minutes later, she returned with a net bag that held new prison clothes. He knew he wasn't due for the clothes or hadn't put in a request, so he figured it to be a mix up that he was receiving them, but didn't say anything. He signed for the clothes and went back to his dormitory.

Back in his cell, he poured the clothes out of the bag and an ounce of weed fell out of the pants. He quickly covered it up and looked at his door, then closed it and covered the window. He started going through the other clothes and found his cell phone inside a pair of socks along with a note from Officer Mitchell, his female friend. He opened the note and read it, and afterwards, he called the number on it. She explained why she hadn't been working his dorm and why she had been acting the way she had towards him. It was all an act. But he received some very troubling news.

After Nard heard about the brutal murder of Mel and his mother, he began cooperating with the detectives. He knew that Huncho had become too powerful and he had no other way of protecting himself other than going to the authorities. Once he began cooperating, he realized that the detectives knew a lot about what was going on between the two cliques. He provided as much information as possible, some real some false, but he made the mistake of identifying Huncho as the shooter that killed Della and caused him to be paralyzed. He figured since Huncho had already been arrested for murder once, it would be an open and shut case. All he had to do was point to him and say, "Yes, he's the one that shot me and killed my girlfriend." And it would be over.

What he didn't know was that Huncho was in Vegas at the time of the shooting and murder. A lot of the things he told the detectives matched what Razor had told them during his anonymous call. They were slowly trying to build a case against him, even though Nard's account of what happened to him could be rebutted.

***

The door to the apartment crashed in and Woadie grabbed his Desert Eagle as he rolled out of his bed. At the sound of movement on the other side of his bedroom door, he began letting out shots shooting through it. Tyra screamed and dove to the floor, curling into a fetal position. Woadie continued firing as chunks were knocked from the door. When he went for his back up pistol on the night stand, the S.W.A.T Team rushed the room. Red beams danced all over his body. He dove to the floor next to his girl as shots began to whistle inches above them, tearing into the walls.

"Clayton County Sheriff Department, put'cha gotdamn hands where I can see them now!" yelled an officer as he crept toward the bed, followed by several more officers aiming an assortment of weapons, some with infrared beams. "Put'cha gotdamn hands up now, muthafucka, now!"

Woadie was lying on top of his girlfriend, covering her. When the door to his apartment crashed in, he didn't know it was 12 because they had come with no warrant to arrest him. Fearing that Tyra would be shot if he made the wrong move, he slowly raised his hands.

"Don't shoot, I'm raising my hands!" he announced.

***

Not far from where Woadie was being arrested, S.W.A.T. was moving in on Bang-Bang's crib along with the Clayton County Fugitive Task Force. They had his spot surrounded, but the only difference from Woadie was that Bang-Bang was wide wake and had seen them coming when he peeked out the window after his neighbors barking pit had got on his nerves. He was snorting cocaine, walking back and forth through the house in a paranoid state, when he had heard the dog. He spotted the marked cruisers and squad cars, he shot to his bedroom and grabbed the MAC11 with the fifty round clip under his pillow and stuck the 45 in his waistband. He was already wearing his bulletproof vest hanging loosely and unstrapped. His heart began to thump rapidly in his chest as he walked quickly back toward the front door, cocking the MAC11. Just as he stepped in the living room, the front and back doors were kicked off the hinges and he opened fire, knocking the first S.W.A.T. member off his feet as he rushed in.

The S.W.A.T. members began firing back and Bang-Bang did nothing to dodge the shots, but instead went towards them with his MAC11 spitting shells from one hand. After pulling the 45 from his waist, he held it beside the MAC as it kicked in his hand.

"Fuck y'all muthafuckas!" he yelled as bullets began hitting his vest, knocking him back. "Y'all can't kill me, bitch! This Bang-Bang!" he added.

The cocaine had his body numb to pain. He was Tony Montana in the flesh. He let off his last few rounds as blood spilled from his mouth. He screamed, continuing on despite his eminent peril like the gangsta he was. He was hit 62 times, but took officers with him, wounding several more. S.W.A.T. team officers approached his body to see that his eyes remained open as if he was staring at them.

***

Huncho got word of the murder warrant and immediately contacted the two lawyers he had on retainer. It was his first time having to use them and they wasted no time coming to his rescue. To say the retainer fee was plenty of money would be an understatement. Before S.W.A.T. and fugitive task force had been sent out to get him, his lawyers had arranged it so that he could turn himself in to the Clayton County headquarters in Jonesboro, and he was escorted in by both attorneys. They'd already talked to him and told him what to expect.

It was much different from the last time he was in an interrogation room being questioned about a murder. This time he knew what and what not to say, he had lawyers, and most of all, he had a rock solid alibi. His lawyers would not allow him to answer questions about anything he wasn't charged with. The only thing he was being charged with was the murder of Della and the shooting of Nard. But as they questioned him about the other murders and his involvement in drugs, he wondered where all of the information had come from. One thing he knew for sure was whoever was doing the talking and snitching was affiliated with the Mafia.

A week later he was released from jail after his lawyers provided the state and investigating detectives with his plane tickets, hotel receipts, pictures, and video footage of him taken and recorded while in Vegas. The state had no choice but to dismiss the investigation and case against him. He had heard about Bang-Bang and Woadie while locked up and had taken Bang-Bang's death kind of hard. Woadie was being held without bond for the murder of Pit, who was killed at the car wash, and seven aggravated assaults on police officers for when he opened fire on S.W.A.T. after they kicked his door in. Since he was Huncho's man, Huncho provided him with his lawyers to fight the cases.

"I've narrowed the shit down, and it can't be nobody but that nigga Razor's bitch ass," Huncho said, as he stared out at the sparkling lake behind his house.

Rock blew out a cloud of smoke that got lost in the wind. "What makes ya think that?" he asked, passing Huncho the blunt.

"Think about it. He said he was at the car wash when the shit happened. Nard wouldn't have known about Woadie chasing the nigga. It was too much detail given about the shooting and the Mafia for it to come from an outsider." Huncho hit the blunt.

"But the fuck nigga Nard had to implicate me because Razor doesn't know the details of the shit that happened to him and the bitch, unless the two been talkin', which I very seriously doubt it," he added. After a moment of silence between the two, he went on to tell him what his lawyers had said about the confidential informant on his case, whose name was being withheld.

They said that as long as the C.I.'s name and identity were being withheld, they couldn't use any of the information against him. Nard's credibility had been destroyed when Huncho had provided a rock solid alibi. He was told to lay low because at any minute, they could charge him if they ever got a material witness that would testify.

After they were done with the blunt, they went back inside Huncho's house and moments later, Rock left.

Huncho laid on the couch in the basement, staring up at the ceiling in deep thought. He felt as if the walls were closing in on him. His partners were dropping dead and getting bammed all around him. His weed connect had been knocked and his coke plug was so hot he couldn't make any moves. Not to mention the murder investigations that were going on, in which his name was too consistent. This in mind, he closed his eyes.

He had money stashed and was loving the new life that it was providing. Where or what had he gone or done wrong, he wondered as he laid on the couch. It was then and there that he realized that it was part of the game. Murder, deceit, and treachery were an everyday thing and occurrence and when you're getting money, it increases the chances tenfold. He saw now that money took the fun out of the game, because everything became more serious. The more money you made, the more serious the game got.

He was brought from his reverie by Zakayla tugging on his shirt for him to lift her up. She had learned how to crawl down the stairs backwards and often came to invade his privacy and chill with him. He looked at her smiled, lifted her in the air, and planted a kiss on her lips before setting her on his chest. As he stared at her, he knew he had some real decisions to make. Live or die, stay free, or go back to prison. He had done what he planned to do, and that was get his money right, but now it was time to implement the next part of his plan before it was too late.

***

Federal Agent Smith and Agent Whitfield were going through hundreds of photos from their surveillance team as well as recorded phone conversations between Huncho, Ricardo, and Carlos. They were trying to build a case against Huncho and find out what part he played in the drug trafficking ring. They had photos of him with the two brothers as well as Purp, all of whom were known drug traffickers. They had recorded phone conservations between the three of them. What they didn't have was him talking about drugs or money. Dealing with the feds, that wasn't needed to get a conviction for conspiracy. All they needed was one muthafucka to implicate him or say his name and it was a wrap. He could get up to a life sentence for conspiracy, and the worst thing about it is he didn't know that they were after him.

"I'm telling you, if we keep digging, we'll find what we're lookin for," Agent Smith said, putting a disk in the CD player. He began listening to a phone conversation between Huncho and Purp. Ricardo and Carlos were still being held in federal custody and had received additional charges for conspiring to have three federal agents murdered so that they couldn't testify against them.

CHAPTER 13

Jerry Killman and Thomas Westbrook were two of the most prominent attorneys in Atlanta associated with the Georgia state bar. They were known as Tom & Jerry in the courtroom and their track record was impeccable. They had fought and won some of the most high profile cases in Georgia.

They were sought after by athletes and people from the music industry that had trouble with the law and their list of clientele included multiplatinum artists and Super Bowl champions. They had made millions.

They pulled up in front of an Italian restaurant called Veni Vidi Vici in Buckhead. They were in Jerry's 5430 Ferrari. He was the more flamboyant of the two and was greeted by the valet parking attendant by name.

"Mr. Killman...Westbrook," the attendant stated with a nod of his head and smile as he was handed the $50 bill for a tip.

"Be careful with her now," Jerry said. "She's a beast."

He and Thomas continued into the restaurant, where reservations had already been made. They had arrived a little early so they could go over case notes together before the arrival of their client. They were led to a private booth and decided to hold off on ordering until the client that they were meeting arrived.

Ten minutes into their conversation, Huncho was escorted to the booth by the hostess. Both lawyers stood in their tailored Armani suits and greeted him with warm smiles and outstretched hands.

"Glad you could make it. Have any trouble finding the place?" Thomas asked as they shook hands.

"No, GPS made it simple," Huncho said, releasing his grip and turning to Jerry. "Mr. Killman."

"Um, could we get menus please, and a bottle of Tori Carver chardonnay?" Jerry requested as he took his seat and watched the maître de disappear.

After they ordered their meals consisting of sword fish, pasta, and rotisserie duck, they got straight down to business. Huncho, from the outside looking in, could have easily been mistaken as a lawyer himself. He was dressed in a Claiborne suit with a $620 shirt by Luigi Borrelli and a pair of $560 dress shoes by Fratelli Rossetti, cufflinks by Salvatore Ferragamo, and a $425 Louis Vuitton belt. He had his short newly twisted dreads professionally done and laid back with a tank Americaine Cartier watch on his wrist.

"We have some good and bad news, and the good news is that you're not going to prison," Jerry said confidently. "Now the bad news is you've made some more enemies that are thorns in the ass to anybody they are after." Huncho looked a little confused and took a sip of chardonnay to shake it off, and Jerry took a sip of his own and then continued. "Your new enemies are known simply as the federal government, or Feds, for short, and you've been in the company of the wrong people."

"First off, they want to know why you were present during an undercover drug buy where kilos cocaine were sold to DEA agents," stated Thomas. "Do you know of a Ricardo and Carlos Espinoza?"

"Yeah, I know 'em, but I don't know nothing about them selling no drugs. I've never seen them in the presence of drugs. So how was I present during a drug buy? I don't understand, they must have the wrong guy," Huncho said.

"Well, do you have a reason for going out to see them? Because they have a copy of your flight record and footage of you boarding and exiting the planes. On each trip, you were being watched the entire time," Jerry said. "I need you to be honest with me because it's my job to get you off. Whether you're guilty or not, I work for you, understand?"

Huncho nodded in agreement as he thought of what he'd been asked. Purp had once told him of the Espinoza brothers secretly owning a couple of studios in Los Angeles and quickly came up with an answer. "What I'm about to say, I don't know if Carlos and Ricardo want it to be known, so I'm telling you this under the client and lawyer privilege."

"Any and everything we ever discuss is always under that privilege," Jerry said.

"Well, they secretly own a couple high profile studios in L.A. I was planning to take my artist out there to record. Before I took my artist out there, I wanted to get to know them and make sure they were about their business. I don't trust just anyone with my artist's career. The music industry is very risky business."

They asked him more questions and he had an answer ready for every one of them. He admitted to a few things, but none that would connect him to Purp and the Espinoza brothers' illegal activities. It was the closest thing to snitching.

After leaving his lawyers, he had to have a drink and a blunt, so he stopped by the liquor store on the way home and bought a bottle of Remy VSOP. He had been warned that the Feds had found a confidential informant that would testify that he had sold bricks of cocaine to him, but the only reason he hadn't been indicted is because the C.I. wasn't able to go before the Federal grand jury yet.

Only one person incapable of making it to a grand jury came to mind.

***

Razor was pulled over in a road block and arrested for possession of a firearm and cocaine. He had been coming from Primetime when he had been stopped. By the time he got to the fourth floor of the Clayton County Detention Center, he went straight to sleep from being tired and coming down off his high.

The next morning the cell doors were open and all of the inmates were forced to sit in the day room so that they couldn't just lay around all day. Razor found a seat under the TV and went back to sleep in one of the hard plastic chairs. He had been getting high on coke for the last week and a half.

He tossed and turned in the chair until he found that right spot and he was off to la la. land. He hadn't been able to sleep much on the street after hearing about Mel and his mother being killed and how they were left. He knew that the Mafia was responsible and that if he were ever caught, something would happen to him. So he stayed high to stay awake or went to a bar or club where he knew he wouldn't be noticed and stayed there until it closed. But now his body screamed for some rest and had shut down. As soon as he found that comfortable spot, he fell into a deep sleep - so deep that he didn't see Woadie sitting at the phone with his back turned.

When Woadie came out of his cell, he went straight to the phone. He didn't associate with any of the other inmates or watch TV, so he passed his time on the phone. He knew that he wasn't getting out anytime soon because bond had been denied until he went before a superior court judge, and he knew that if he did get one, he would never be able to make it, his lawyers had said. He knew Huncho had spent good money on the lawyers he had. He had given the money that he had stashed to help also. But so far, the lawyers had been talking good, using a self-defense claim for firing at the S.W.A.T. members who entered his home without announcing themselves. Even though the no knock warrant was valid, the lawyers said a man still had a right to protect himself and there was no way he could have known that it was S.W.A.T. members he was shooting at when he had been in his bed asleep when the door was kicked in.

A witness still hadn't stepped forth for the murder of Pit at the car wash. All the detectives had was a blurry video that showed two black males with dreads chasing another that had been captured by a camera on a pole. The video was so blurry there was no way anyone could say that he was one of the people in it. Tom and Jerry told him to just relax and let them work the cases.

After making three phone calls, he got up from the stool and stretched. At first he thought that his eyes were playing tricks on him when he spotted Razor sleeping in the chair. He had pulled both of his arms inside of his red county jail top, keeping warm, leaving himself totally defenseless. Woadie eased closer to get a better look, to make sure it was Razor. He had already determined along with his Mafia brothers that Razor was responsible for him being locked up and Camry's kidnapping. Once he confirmed that it was Razor, he wasted no time in getting to business.

He grabbed a mop wringer by the handle and snatched it from the bucket. Other inmates looked on in silence and no one attempted to stop him. He casually walked up to Razor and brought the mop wringer down on his head, causing blood to skeet on the inmate that sitting next to him.

"Wake up, bitch-ass nigga!" he said, bringing the wringer down again. "Run tell this, wit'cha punk ass!"

Razor slid out of the chair, never knowing what hit him. He went into convulsions on the floor and his eyes rolled back in his head, as his body shook.

Woadie pulled a shank from under his shirt and tossed it next to Razor, who was bleeding worse than a stuck hog.

"This nigga a muthafuckin' snitch, and he tried to stab me when 12 ask what happen," he added to convince the other inmates that Razor was a snitch and to go along with his self-defense claim.

Officers stormed the dorm and after locking everyone down, they rushed an unconscious Razor out on the medical cart with his head bandaged. When inmates were asked what happened, they all said they didn't know or that Woadie was defending himself from the other inmate that had tried to stab him.

***

Federal Agent Smith had remained persistent in listening to the hundreds of hours of phone conversations that had been recorded of the Espinoza brothers, Purp, and Huncho. He would ride around with a CD in his disc player instead of listening to music. While sitting in the office, he would listen to the CD's. Some nights he left his wife in bed asleep while he got up at two or three o'clock in the morning, unable to sleep, thinking about the cases.

He knew there was something there. All he needed was one tiny slip up and he knew the United States District Attorney would turn it into a conviction. There was no way possible out of all the phone conversations recorded that neither one had slipped up. He thought it couldn't be possible, He had been in the business for over twenty years and hadn't seen it yet. True to his gut feeling, he finally found what he was looking for.

"Aye, papi, this Yara," a female's voice said. "Your boy Huncho is over here and he brought the paperwork, but he brought some extra contracts and said he wanted to lay his own track this time."

"Get the contracts from him and tell 'em I said deduct it from the tracks he's getting now, and we'll discuss the other contracts when I get back in town," Purp had said, and then the line went dead.

Agent Whitfield played it over and over until he memorized the call word for word, and he knew that they had to be talking about drugs and money in code. He just had to decipher it. Now he had to find out who the Spanish chick Yara was so that he could scare her up.

***

Huncho knew that his time was running out despite what the lawyers had said. The Feds had a 98% conviction rate, so that meant damn near everybody they went at, they got. He hadn't ever seen a nigga beat them yet that didn't snitch or take the stand against another nigga. If that was the only way to beat 'em, he knew he was fucked and up shit's creek, because there was no way he was breaking the code.

He had figured out that Nard was trying to get him indicted as a way of revenge since accusing him of the shooting failed. He knew if Nard ever made it to the grand jury and testified that he had served him some work, regardless of how true or false it was, he was through. An indictment in the Feds meant the same thing as a guilty verdict and the 98% conviction rate proved it, so there was no way that he could let Nard live any longer. But he had one problem. His two killers were gone.

Bang-Bang was dead and Woadie was in the County. Rock had been laying low since the Nard shooting and there was no one else he trusted enough. But then a thought popped up in his mind. He didn't know if it would work or not, but he had to give it a try.

***

"Huncho, have you lost your damn mind?" Camry asked with anger in her voice. "Please tell me you are high and just trippin'!"

"Look, baby, the shit isn't what you think, but if this nigga testify, I'm finished. It's just like he killing me 'cause I'm gone. Won't be no winning no appeal this time!" he honestly added.

"Huncho, I can't believe you're askin' me to do some stupid shit like that!" she shouted. "Why don't you ask one of your goons? They've been killing for you, haven't they!" Tears were streaming down her cheeks, her arms crossed over her chest.

Huncho released a deep sigh, got up from the couch, and began pacing back and forth. He knew he had to make a move fast. Time was running out. Camry had reacted just as he suspected she would, but he knew he had to convince her to help him. He stopped pacing and sat beside her, where she sat crying on the couch. Seeing her cry made him feel bad, but he put his feelings aside.

"I know it's a fucked up situation. I know it sounds crazy. I know, but you all I got right now," he said, as he looked into her watering eyes. "And don't get me wrong, I do feel bad for comin' at you like this, but baby, it is what it is. You know it ain't nothin' in the world I wouldn't do for you and you the only I can trust. I want to be here to see Zakayla grow up and our son born, but if this nigga makes it to them folks, it's a wrap, baby, I'm gone again."

Camry began crying harder and he took her into his arms and held her in silence. As she cried, he rubbed her back and stroked her hair. All types of things were going through his mind, but only one of them mattered, and that was killing Nard so he couldn't make it to testify before the Grand Jury.

***

Purp hopped out of his black Rolls Royce Phantom with his phone pressed to his ear, face twisted in an angry snarl, as he listened to the caller on the other end. He stepped into Club 5-4-3 and went straight to his office, signaling a waitress to fix him a drink as he passed the bar. On the other end of the phone was his lawyer, who was telling him about the phone call that the Feds were trying to use to get him and Huncho indicted on conspiracy charges.

"Have you heard the call yourself yet?" Purp asked as he sat behind his desk and put his feet on the desk.

"Not yet, but I'm working my ass off to get a copy of it," his lawyer said. "But they're being asses about releasing it until the Grand Jury hears it."

"This is bullshit, Scott!" Purp replied, "You know them muthafuckas stay fuckin' with me, and now they're real desperate since they've got some guys that I know and do music with. So what is the call supposed to be about?"

"Some Spanish chick supposed to been conducting a drug deal over the phone for you and some guy named Huncho and-"

"Huncho!" Purp gasped. "Get the fuck out of here, Scott! Me and him have never talked about any fuckin' drugs! Just another guy connected through the music – well, he's just gettin' started and we've been workin' together. He uses my studio, and our artists collaborated on a few tracks together. Nothin' more, nothin' less, Scott." Purp waved for the waitress to enter his office.

He knew exactly what call his lawyer was talking about, because he had addressed Yara for using Huncho's name on the phone. He was glad Huncho had been smart enough not to make the call himself, because without his voice actually recorded during the phone call, the Feds would have trouble getting them indicted unless…

"They went at Yara!" He quickly wrapped up the call with his attorney, cutting him off mid-sentence. "Look, Scott, we'll have to continue this later. Something just come up that requires my attention!" He rose to his feet and rushed out his office, downing his drink in one gulp.

He jumped in the Phantom coupe and pulled out his burnout phone that couldn't be traced and quickly dialed Yara's number. He bent the corner, ignoring the stop sign, and mashed on the gas, causing the big luxury car to lunge forward. Yara finally picked up the phone on the fifth ring, sounding as though she had been in a deep sleep, still hung over from the partying the night before.

"Hello." Her voice was dry and groggy. "What's up, papi?"

"Get up and pack ya bags, ASAP! I'm on my way to get you!" Purp ended the call without another word.

He whipped the Phantom in and out of traffic as if it was a race car. After turning on expressway 285, he picked the burn out phone back up and called the Marquis Jet which he often used to travel back and forth across the map. He had a prepaid flight card with 100 hours on it and he was about to use some of them to get his girl out of the country before the Feds got to her.

What he didn't know was the Feds were following from the sky. A helicopter was watching his every move, giving the ground his location so they could stay out of sight, undetected.

CHAPTER 14

Nard awoke in the middle of the night, unable to sleep. It had been like that every day since he had talked to the federal agents and told them about Huncho. He had implicated himself with promised immunity when he fabricated the story about buying bricks from Huncho and Southside Mafia. After the attempt failed to get him arrested for shooting him and killing Della, he knew that he had to get Huncho off the streets for sure. He had exposed his hand.

He knew his days in the game were over with. He would never walk again. The doctors said there was one more surgery they could try to get him back on his feet, but he would be risking being paralyzed from the neck down if the surgery failed. He thought about it a couple days and decided to roll the dice to do it. If it worked, he walked, and if it didn't, he would be in the same position, bound to a wheelchair for the rest of his life.

The surgery was scheduled for the following morning and he was kind of nervous about it. He laid in bed thinking on his life experiences. How hundreds of thousands of dollars had been through his hands. He had fucked some of the baddest bitches a nigga could dream of. Niggas did what he said, and envied him all the same while others tried to emulate his swag.

But as he laid there in the dimly-lit room in silence, he wondered if his perfidious ways had come back on him to leave him paralyzed. He had crossed his crew to free himself, then started his own. Even after starting his own mafia, he continued on with his cutthroat, disloyal ways. He would front them work, then rob them so they would be in debt. That scheme alone had made him prosper in the game and rise quicker than others.

He thought of the first time he had done it to his homeboy JT. He gave JT a half a brick to hold at his crib while they went to the club. What JT didn't know was it was a set up the whole time. Nard had removed his house key from his key ring a couple days earlier, and had it duplicated, and put it back with the others on the ring, unbeknownst to JT. While out clubbing, he had his nephew run up in JT's house and get the work and whatever else they wanted. When they returned and Nard asked for the work and JT couldn't produce, he went into a rage and pulled his gun out, accusing JT of stealing from him. Nard threatened to kill him and JT pleaded for his life, removing his jewelry and money from his pocket, offering it to Nard as collateral until he could reimburse him for the half a brick while Nard rose to the top and became his boss.

"Oh, you're up, Mr. Evans." A nurse came into his room, toting a tray. "I just need to check your vitals and get some blood samples, okay? Feeling okay, today?"

"Yeah, but my back been bothering me and I can't sleep."

"Well, I read your chart and know you're probably experiencing some pain from all of the surgeries and injuries and I'm not supposed to give you anything other than what the doctor ordered," the nurse said, before looking both ways in a dramatic gesture. She winked at him, and lowered her voice a few octaves. "So you can't tell anyone."

Nard put his hand up to his mouth, acted as if he was zipping his lips shut, and smiled. The nurse went on to take his vitals and set the call button and remote on the table next to his bed so she could get the sedative shot she was about to give him. She pulled out a needle then walked over to the door of the room and looked out to make sure no one was coming before she went back to the bed. As she placed the needle into his arm, her hands slightly shook. When he looked up at her, he saw that her eyes had begun to water as she shot the fluid into his veins.

"Huncho said hello," she mumbled before spinning on her heels and quickly exiting the room.

Nard's eyes bucked and he attempted to reach for the call button that she had moved out of his reach. Camry had shot him up with sodium hydroxide. The lethal fluid shot through his veins, and invaded his respiratory system. He felt as if he was under water and drowning, and then his heart exploded in his chest so that he could never unzip his lips.

By the time Camry walked out of the hospital in the nurse uniform that she worked in, she was sobbing.

Huncho pulled up to the sidewalk and opened the door for her, then they rode off like Bonnie and Clyde.

***

When the Hawker 400xp landed in Santo Domingo, Yara's eyes began to water again. She had not wanted to return to her West Indies home on the island of Hispaniola. She wanted to stay with Purp in America. She cried even more for the reason she had to flee the country, feeling it was her fault and she had failed Purp. He had told her time and time again to never use names on the phone and now it was costing her.

Of course she would continue to live good until she returned to the states because Purp had provided her with two hefty traveler checks and promised to wire her more whenever she needed it. That wasn't enough to make her want to stay, though. Yara came from money. Her uncle was beyond wealthy, and had been since she could remember, though he opted to continue his dealings within law enforcement. Why, was beyond her, but she had been well taken care of before she even knew a Purp existed, something he was unaware of himself until she confided in him her family secret. And till this day, he still treated her the same. He took care of her, despite her background, refusing all help from her uncle, stressing adamantly that a man's purpose was to provide and protect his family and those of whom he loves. All the same, it was something he chose to do. Outside of his devotion, she never "needed" Purp for anything. She was in love with a gangsta, and simply wanted to prove to him, without contradiction, that no other woman could be a greater asset to him on any level. Now all she wanted was to be with her man, where she felt she was needed now more than ever. There was no way she was going to sit back and allow another bitch to take her place. Naw, fuck that shit! She was going back to reclaim her rightful place on the throne, where she belonged.

She descended the exit ramp of the luxury jet and was met at the bottom by two uniformed officers and a very important-looking gentleman wearing plain clothes. She knew in an instant that it meant trouble.

"Ms. Santiago, would you please come with us?" the plain-clothed gentleman said.

***

Nard's body was found in his room and was quickly ruled a suspicious death. They were waiting for the autopsy and toxicology reports from the medical examiner's office.

Camry hadn't spoken to Huncho since she agreed to do it, and ever since she had, all she did was cry. She couldn't sleep and hadn't been to work or school either. In fact, she had quit her job and abandoned her medical career altogether. There was no way she could ever put on nurse scrubs or pick up a needle after what she had done.

Huncho had tried to comfort her, but she rejected his advances. She was unable to look at him when he entered the room and was glad when he was gone away from the house. She had taken another person's life and felt hers would never be the same again. She tried rationalizing the situation, telling herself Huncho would have done it for her. That she knew without a doubt. But she wasn't a killer, thug, or goon. She was just in love with all of the above. So taking someone else's life wasn't an easy pill to swallow.

Huncho, on the other hand, went on as if nothing had ever happened, telling Camry they had no choice. Nard would've taken him away from her and the kids. He knew there was no way Camry would or could be caught. They had taken extra precautions to conceal her identity, not only by drastically changing her appearance, but also by strategically avoiding all security cameras.

Nard was out of the way, and Huncho was once again showing his face on the Southside. It had been a few days since Nard's enigmatic murder, and with him out of the way, he had no worries. But that quickly changed when Purp called him about the phone call the Feds were trying to use.

He knew he hadn't talked business over the phone with Purp, especially not illegal business. Ever! Nevertheless, the mention of it didn't sit well with him. He was already being investigated for being associated with the Espinoza brothers, who were also connected to Purp.

He pulled into Ms. Ann's and got out of his Escalade, then headed in to get one of the famous Ghetto Burgers that she made. He was in good spirits as he walked to the door, floating on a cloud from the blunt he had just smoked. As he reached the door, two females were on their way out, laughing at something a short, stocky guy had said to them. Both were attractive, and they had his undivided attention as he held the door open for them to exit.

"Ain't your name Huncho?" the darker of the two wanted to know.

"Depends on the benefits of my response." He was locked in and the intensity was reciprocal.

"You be with my cousin Rock. My name is Crystal." She smiled hard, revealing a nice set of pearly whites. "When you see 'em, tell him he needs to call me, and here, give him my new number." She removed a pen and a wrinkled Subway napkin from her purse, jotted down her number, and handed it over.

"I'll do that." He took her number and watched as she and her friend walked off, admiring their curvaceous assets. Shaking his head, he stepped into the crowded snack bar. After ordering his ghetto burger, he called Rock and talked to him while he waited for his food. When he told him about bumping into his cousin, Rock busted out laughing.

"Man, that girl just saw me yesterday and she's had the same number since cell phones came out!" He laughed again. "She think she got all the mu'fuckin' sense!"

"Who's the pretty li'l brown one that was with her? She was dumb bad. You know her?" Huncho half-yelled over the noise resulting from the many conversations surrounding him.

"Shanika, most likely. Heard she used to dance at one point," Rock said. "As a matter of fact, she the one identified Mel. Saw the whole thing on a humbug."

"Oh yeah, that's where I remember her face from." A group of friends walked by behind him, laughing. "I thought she moved out of town or something."

"She did, until Mel got clapped. She just moved back recently."

Huncho's line beeped. He looked at the caller ID and saw that it was Purp. "Aye, say, Rock, let me hit you back. I need to take this call." He clicked over to Purp, who instructed him to bring Dreak to the studio for a session, but he knew what he really wanted. They chopped music for a few before ending the call. Huncho left to scoop Dreak.

***

"You're ready to talk, I see, Mr. Espinoza?" Agent Smith was sitting across from a handcuffed and shackled Carlos. They were alone in an ice-cold, florescent-lit interrogation room.

"It depends." Carlos's tone was flat, as if he was in total control of the conversation.

"Depends on what?" Smith shot back, keeping his game face on.

"…on what you can do for me. Ya know, scratch my back, I scratch yours." Carlos raised an eyebrow and hunched his shoulders.

Agent Smith savored the moment, as he always did. There was nothing like seeing one of the guys he had been after for years break, at long last in need of his help. It always put him in the power seat, the silent surrender that clearly said he could get exactly what he wanted regardless of his ability to provide the snitch any relief whatsoever. He had been down this road over a thousand times with some of the most perfidious criminals known to America, from stone cold killers to the nation's most renown drug traffickers. They were 'Bout It 'Bout It", all right, but when it came time to man up, this is what most resorted to.

Telling.

"Well, Mr. Espinoza, it's not looking good for you. As of now, you're fucked, you know," Smith said. "You've sold over a hundred kilos to federal agents, then arranged to have them killed to prevent them from testifying against you and your brother. As of now, you're looking at life plus in Florence ADX, at the minimum. So if you want me to scratch your back, you have to give me something really good to make the D.A. happy enough to change his mind."

Carlos dropped his head for a second and then looked back up as Whitfield entered, posting up by the door. Whitfield didn't so much as blink.

Carlos had been thinking long and hard about what he was about to do, and now the moment had come. It went against what he believed in, was raised on, and everything he stood for, but he just wasn't built for prison. He knew he would never see the streets again with all the evidence the federal government had against him. Maybe Ricardo could handle it, but he knew for sure he couldn't.

"I'll give him whatever he needs if he will go easy on me," he finally answered.

Smith and Whitfield nearly cracked a smile. "I want names, dates, places, and all the specifics," Smith said. "If it all adds up, I'll go to the district attorney on your behalf. But if you bullshit me, so help me God, I'll be the one personally escorting you to Colorado super maximum security prison."

For the next hour and a half he listened to Carlos, questioning him every so often for clarity.

***

After setting Dreak up with 5-4-3 Studio's Audio Engineer, Purp and Huncho went to another part of the studio, exiting a door. He hadn't trusted talking in the studio ever since the Feds had been on the inside, figuring more than likely that they had planted bugs during their search. Huncho could tell something was on his mind and as they stepped out the door, he hoped it wasn't nothing he didn't already know.

"They got Yara, my G." Purp pulled a Newport box from his pocket, removed one, and lit up, then blew out the smoke. "I flew her out the country, but some way they peeped the move. They were waiting for her in the Santo Domingo. Snatched her as soon as she got off the plane."

"Think she'll say anything to hurt you?" Huncho left himself out, purposely, thinking street. When the Feds were involved, everyone was suspect.

"Shiiid, the Feds can break the strong. Have done so in the past, and probably will continue to do so, you can bet your last dime on that. They play the game real raw, feel me?" Purp hit the cigarette, scrutinizing Huncho with narrowed eyes. He hadn't missed the way in which the question was asked, but he was unsure if Huncho was playing it safe or setting him up. "I'm waitin' on her people to holla back at me. They trying to pull some strings before they send her back to the states. By law, they can only hold her for so long without charging her. That's a good thing. Another card in our favor is her uncle's political there. I'm tryna see how much it'll take to get her out, now."

They continued talking for a good ten minutes, both guarded with their words. Just as they were about to step in the studio, Purp's phone rang. He answered and listened to the caller and Huncho saw his face change from whatever news he was getting from the caller. He looked at Huncho and held up one finger as his face twisted in anger. He listened for a few more seconds before slowly bringing the phone from his ear.

"That was Ricardo's wife. She said Carlos turned state witness," he said.

"Damn, that's fucked up. He snitchin' on his own brother?" Huncho's face was of pure disbelief.

"There's more. He's sayin' me and you his suppliers, G. He's going before the grand jury to testify," Purp said. Then they stared at each other, lost for words.

"Yo requrir hasta matar suyo niña, amiga y carbrites y yo quiere tener suyo garganta cortad," Ricardo whispered to his oldest son Pedro, telling him to kill Carlos's girlfriend and kids, and that he would have Carlos's throat cut.

Twenty-two-year-old Dinero gave a slight nod, looking into his father's eyes. Ricardo found out Carlos had been secretly meeting with the Feds and had his lawyers do an immediate investigation. He believed in death before dishonor, so before Carlos dishonored the Espinoza name, he would die first.

That's if he could be got to in time!

To Be Continued...
Triggadale 3
Coming Soon

Submission Guideline

Submit the first three chapters of your completed manuscript to ldpsubmissions@gmail.com, subject line: Your book's title. The manuscript must be in a .doc file and sent as an attachment. Document should be in Times New Roman, double spaced and in size 12 font. Also, provide your synopsis and full contact information. If sending multiple submissions, they must each be in a separate email.

Have a story but no way to send it electronically? You can still submit to LDP/Ca$h Presents. Send in the first three chapters, written or typed, of your completed manuscript to:

LDP: Submissions Dept
Po Box 870494
Mesquite, Tx 75187

DO NOT send original manuscript. Must be a duplicate.

Provide your synopsis and a cover letter containing your full contact information.

Thanks for considering LDP and Ca$h Presents.

Coming Soon from Lock Down Publications/Ca$h Presents

BOW DOWN TO MY GANGSTA

By **Ca$h**

TORN BETWEEN TWO

By **Coffee**

BLOOD STAINS OF A SHOTTA **III**

By **Jamaica**

STEADY MOBBIN **III**

By **Marcellus Allen**

BLOOD OF A BOSS **VI**

By **Askari**

LOYAL TO THE GAME **IV**

LIFE OF SIN **III**

By **T.J. & Jelissa**

A DOPEBOY'S PRAYER **II**

By **Eddie "Wolf" Lee**

IF LOVING YOU IS WRONG… **III**

LOVE ME EVEN WHEN IT HURTS **III**

By **Jelissa**

TRUE SAVAGE **VII**

By **Chris Green**

BLAST FOR ME **III**

DUFFLE BAG CARTEL **IV**

By **Ghost**

ADDICTIED TO THE DRAMA **III**

By **Jamila Mathis**

A HUSTLER'S DECEIT 3

KILL ZONE **II**

BAE BELONGS TO ME III

SOUL OF A MONSTER II

By **Aryanna**

THE COST OF LOYALTY **III**

By **Kweli**

SHE FELL IN LOVE WITH A REAL ONE **II**

By **Tamara Butler**

RENEGADE BOYS **III**

By **Meesha**

CORRUPTED BY A GANGSTA **IV**

By **Destiny Skai**

A GANGSTER'S SYN II

By **J-Blunt**

KING OF NEW YORK V

RISE TO POWER III

COKE KINGS III

By **T.J. Edwards**

GORILLAZ IN THE BAY III

De'Kari

THE STREETS ARE CALLING II

Duquie Wilson

KINGPIN KILLAZ IV

STREET KINGS 2

PAID IN BLOOD 2

Hood Rich

SINS OF A HUSTLA II

ASAD

TRIGGADALE III

Elijah R. Freeman

MARRIED TO A BOSS III

By Destiny Skai & Chris Green

KINGZ OF THE GAME III

Playa Ray

SLAUGHTER GANG II

By Willie Slaughter

THE HEART OF A SAVAGE II

By Jibril Williams

FUK SHYT II

By Blakk Diamond

THE DOPEMAN'S BODYGAURD II

By Tranay Adams

Available Now

RESTRAINING ORDER **I & II**

By **CA$H & Coffee**

LOVE KNOWS NO BOUNDARIES **I II & III**

By **Coffee**

RAISED AS A GOON I, II, III & IV

BRED BY THE SLUMS I, II, III

BLAST FOR ME I & II

ROTTEN TO THE CORE I II III

A BRONX TALE I, II, III

DUFFEL BAG CARTEL I II III

By **Ghost**

LAY IT DOWN **I & II**

LAST OF A DYING BREED

BLOOD STAINS OF A SHOTTA I & II

By **Jamaica**

LOYAL TO THE GAME

LOYAL TO THE GAME II

LOYAL TO THE GAME III

LIFE OF SIN I, II

By **TJ & Jelissa**

BLOODY COMMAS I & II

SKI MASK CARTEL I II & III

KING OF NEW YORK I II,III IV

RISE TO POWER I II

COKE KINGS I II

By **T.J. Edwards**

IF LOVING HIM IS WRONG…I & II

LOVE ME EVEN WHEN IT HURTS I II

By **Jelissa**

WHEN THE STREETS CLAP BACK I & II III

By **Jibril Williams**

A DISTINGUISHED THUG STOLE MY HEART I II & III

LOVE SHOULDN'T HURT I II III IV

RENEGADE BOYS I & II

By **Meesha**

A GANGSTER'S CODE I &, II III

A GANGSTER'S SYN

By J-Blunt

PUSH IT TO THE LIMIT

By **Bre' Hayes**

BLOOD OF A BOSS **I, II, III, IV, V**

By **Askari**

THE STREETS BLEED MURDER **I, II & III**

THE HEART OF A GANGSTA I II& III

By **Jerry Jackson**

CUM FOR ME

CUM FOR ME 2

CUM FOR ME 3

CUM FOR ME 4

An **LDP Erotica Collaboration**

BRIDE OF A HUSTLA **I II & II**

THE FETTI GIRLS **I, II& III**

CORRUPTED BY A GANGSTA I, II & III

By **Destiny Skai**

WHEN A GOOD GIRL GOES BAD

By **Adrienne**

THE COST OF LOYALTY

By Kweli

A GANGSTER'S REVENGE **I II III & IV**

THE BOSS MAN'S DAUGHTERS

THE BOSS MAN'S DAUGHTERS II

THE BOSSMAN'S DAUGHTERS III

THE BOSSMAN'S DAUGHTERS IV

THE BOSS MAN'S DAUGHTERS **V**

A SAVAGE LOVE **I & II**

BAE BELONGS TO ME I II

A HUSTLER'S DECEIT I, II, III

WHAT BAD BITCHES DO I, II, III

SOUL OF A MONSTER

By **Aryanna**

A KINGPIN'S AMBITON

A KINGPIN'S AMBITION **II**

I MURDER FOR THE DOUGH

By **Ambitious**

TRUE SAVAGE

TRUE SAVAGE II

TRUE SAVAGE **III**

TRUE SAVAGE **IV**

TRUE SAVAGE **V**

TRUE SAVAGE **VI**

By **Chris Green**

A DOPEBOY'S PRAYER

By **Eddie "Wolf" Lee**

THE KING CARTEL **I, II & III**

By **Frank Gresham**

THESE NIGGAS AIN'T LOYAL **I, II & III**

By **Nikki Tee**

GANGSTA SHYT **I II &III**

By **CATO**

THE ULTIMATE BETRAYAL

By **Phoenix**

BOSS'N UP **I , II & III**

By **Royal Nicole**

I LOVE YOU TO DEATH

By Destiny J

I RIDE FOR MY HITTA

I STILL RIDE FOR MY HITTA

By **Misty Holt**

LOVE & CHASIN' PAPER

By **Qay Crockett**

TO DIE IN VAIN

SINS OF A HUSTLA

By **ASAD**

BROOKLYN HUSTLAZ

By **Boogsy Morina**

BROOKLYN ON LOCK I & II

By **Sonovia**

GANGSTA CITY

By **Teddy Duke**

A DRUG KING AND HIS DIAMOND I & II III

A DOPEMAN'S RICHES

HER MAN, MINE'S TOO I, II

CASH MONEY HO'S

By Nicole Goosby

TRAPHOUSE KING **I II & III**

KINGPIN KILLAZ I II III

STREET KINGS

PAID IN BLOOD

By **Hood Rich**

LIPSTICK KILLAH **I, II, III**

CRIME OF PASSION I & II

By **Mimi**

STEADY MOBBN' **I, II, III**

By **Marcellus Allen**

WHO SHOT YA **I, II, III**

Renta

GORILLAZ IN THE BAY **I II**

DE'KARI

TRIGGADALE I II

Elijah R. Freeman

GOD BLESS THE TRAPPERS I, II, III

THESE SCANDALOUS STREETS I, II, III

FEAR MY GANGSTA I, II, III

THESE STREETS DON'T LOVE NOBODY I, II

BURY ME A G I, II, III, IV, V

A GANGSTA'S EMPIRE I, II, III, IV

THE DOPEMAN'S BODYGAURD

Tranay Adams

THE STREETS ARE CALLING

Duquie Wilson

MARRIED TO A BOSS… I II

By Destiny Skai & Chris Green

<u>KINGZ OF THE GAME I II</u>

Playa Ray

<u>SLAUGHTER GANG II</u>

By Willie Slaughter

<u>THE HEART OF A SAVAGE</u>

By Jibril Williams

FUK SHYT

By Blakk Diamond

BOOKS BY LDP'S CEO, CA$H

TRUST IN NO MAN

TRUST IN NO MAN 2

TRUST IN NO MAN 3

BONDED BY BLOOD

SHORTY GOT A THUG

THUGS CRY

THUGS CRY 2

THUGS CRY 3

TRUST NO BITCH

TRUST NO BITCH 2

TRUST NO BITCH 3

TIL MY CASKET DROPS

RESTRAINING ORDER

RESTRAINING ORDER 2

IN LOVE WITH A CONVICT

Coming Soon

BONDED BY BLOOD 2

BOW DOWN TO MY GANGSTA

CPSIA information can be obtained
at www.ICGtesting.com
Printed in the USA
BVHW080213190819
556172BV00014B/1321/P